Falling for Red

A High Five Novella
Book #5

By Serena Pier

Jake Schmidt looks Republican. Fortunately for all of us, he identifies as a pleasure Dom.

Reading Order

It is encouraged, but not required to have read the first four novellas in the High Five Novella Series before reading Falling for Red.

High Five Novella **Series:**

Part 1

Santa's Coming
Cupid's Shot
Shamrock Kisses

Part 2

Run, Little Bunny
Falling For Red
Sharing Shadow Secrets (Releasing September 25th)

Content Warning

This book contains themes that may not be suitable to some readers. Please read with care.

Trigger warnings: alcohol consumption, profanity, sexually explicit scenes, discussion of authority figures and politics, discussions of racism, discussions of past military service, mentions of parental death (off page), discussions of narcissistic abuse, past cheating and divorce, self worth issues, and mild BDSM themes.

1

Claire

Tuesday, July 1st

"I can't leave work right now," I tell the daycare attendant and tighten the grip of my phone. Glancing at the handful of happy hour regulars, I add, "I'm the only one at the bar."

Tuesdays at High Five, a reformed small town dive bar in Lake Geneva, Wisconsin, are never slammed. This place is welcoming with newly renovated wood floors and a cozy vibe. It's what drew me in to apply. When I'm bartending, the music is always low, so I don't have to yell over it. My noon to six shift has a nice flow, making it worth my time. I can run the place all by myself as long as no one decides to be an asshole.

"She has a fever." The attendant's voice is insistent because yes, I know. If you have a fever, you have to go home. Gabby rarely gets sick though. Closing my eyes, I shake my head at the impossible situation.

"I'll be there as soon as I can." I sigh loudly, leaning

against the wood bar. It's a little after four now. Hopefully, one of the other bartenders can come in early.

I dial Aaron Olson, the manager, silently praying.

"Hey, what's going on?" he answers, his voice laced with concern. I've never called him about needing to leave work early, but I understand the unease in his voice. The only time I call Aaron during my shift is to tell him about an incident—like a drunk throwing a punch.

"Gabby has a fever. I need to pick her up."

"Of course." There's a pause, and then he says, "I can be there in a few minutes."

Exhaling, I feel a rush of gratitude. I'm lucky to be working in a place that gets it—that people have lives. Everyone in Wisconsin is nice, definitely nicer than the people I've worked with in Chicago.

"That's—"

The screech of a fire alarm cuts me off, piercing through the bar's noise. A collective gasp ripples through the crowd as people start looking around.

"What's going on?" Aaron's voice is faint over the blaring sound.

"I don't know!" I yell back, not seeing anything out of the ordinary, but then I smell the scent of smoke. My gaze darts around the bar. If there is a fire, maybe it's in the bathrooms? I round the corner of the bar to investigate. Since I began working here, that's happened a handful of times—people smoking in the bathrooms.

"Shit!" I scream after yanking open the women's bathroom door. One of the garbage cans is ablaze. Flames are climbing up the wall.

I hang up on Aaron and frantically dial 911. My hands shake as I turn on the sink and dampen a wad of paper towels, tossing them into the fire.

"911. Where's your emergency?" a woman's voice asks.

"There's a fire at High Five, the bar on Main Street," I shout into the phone, my breath coming in ragged gasps. The heat is oppressive, and panic grips my chest as the flames grow.

Fire extinguisher! I drop my phone on the bathroom sink and sprint back to the bar where we keep one. I can't wait for help; I need to put out this fire now.

2

Jake

"Time to shine," I shout to the guys, adrenaline already kicking in. A real fire. Not a cat in a tree or something small—an actual fire. In the station, we suit up fast.

"Let's go, January," I tease the oldest member of our crew while pushing back my blond hair and putting on my fire helmet. He's still tying his boots, and the rest of us are ready to go. I don't want to be like him, fighting fires when I'm approaching fifty, but I love this job and serving the community.

"I'm moving, August," he shoots back, and I chuckle. Ever since our calendar fundraiser, these new nicknames have taken hold.

"September, December, January." I nod at the guys as they pile into the truck. "Two minutes out," I call over the radio, stepping in. The truck zooms down the quiet small-town streets, sirens blaring.

High Five. My buddy's bar. Everyone in this town has at least one good and one regrettable memory at High Five. It's a staple here in Lake Geneva, and Nicholas has kept the charm while pouring money into renovating the place since he bought it last year. We can't let it burn down.

As we pull up, a crowd has already gathered outside. A dozen or so people are standing around the brick building, and all eyes turn to us. I jump out. "Anyone inside?" I shout.

"Claire," a guy says.

Claire? Why the hell is someone still inside?

We move quickly, rushing into the bar. It's eerily quiet, the stillness feeling wrong for a place like High Five. Most nights it's impossible to find a bar stool. I spot smoke in the back corner and gesture to the guys. Without words, we head toward it. Pushing open the bathroom door, I spot her —red hair falling around her face, sitting next to an overturned trash can, a fire extinguisher still in hand. The can is covered in that familiar white, chalky powder.

She scowls as soon as she sees me, her blue eyes meeting mine. "Took you long enough."

I blink, caught off guard, staring down at her. "You didn't have to do our job for us," I joke, pointing to the mess.

"Well, someone had to." She crosses her arms, one brow arching.

I huff out a laugh, more impressed than I probably should be by this sassy, short woman. "Are you Claire?"

"Yes."

"Good. Let's get you outside."

"I'm fine." She waves me off, standing and stepping around the extinguisher residue like this is just another Tuesday.

I block her exit. "Smoke inhalation isn't something to brush off. You need to get checked out."

She rolls her eyes. "I barely breathed in any smoke. I'm fine."

I've never seen her around town. Intrigued, I need to refocus. "It's protocol. You have to be evaluated."

Claire gives me a long, measuring look, then lets out an exaggerated sigh. "Fine."

Outside, I look for the ambulance but don't see it. I part the growing crowd as I guide her to the truck. People are always too nosey at the scene, standing too close to us while we try to work. I softly smile and gesture to the bumper. "Sit."

"You're bossy." She plops down but glares at me like she's doing me a favor.

"It's my job." I motion for a space blanket, but before I can wrap it around her, she grabs it and does it herself.

"I need to go," she mutters, already pushing up to her feet.

I step in front of her, nearly placing my hand on her shoulder. "No," I say, maybe too seriously. "You need to wait for the ambulance."

Her big blue eyes search mine before she exhales sharply. "I don't have time for this. My daughter is sick, and I need to pick her up."

I soften slightly at the mention of her daughter, but I have to hold my ground and do my job. "Can you call someone? I can't let you leave."

Her jaw clenches. "You can't let me leave?" She folds her arms. "Didn't realize I was under arrest."

I bite back a smirk. "You're not. But you inhaled smoke, and protocol says you have to stay put."

She throws her head back, groaning.

"Claire." We both turn at the sound of a familiar voice. Aaron Olson jogs up, his expression tight with concern.

"Hey," I say. I've known him for years. We're not close friends, but we've gotten along since he was a freshman on the wrestling team when I was a senior. Looking at him, you'd never know he wrestled at the lowest weight class. Dude is jacked. He's been working at High Five for years now, and Nicholas made him the manager earlier this year.

"I need to get Gabby," Claire says, her voice shifting into something more urgent.

I glance at Aaron. "She has to be evaluated first."

Aaron looks between us, then nods at Claire. "I can get her."

Claire presses her fingers to her temples like she's exasperated, but I catch the flicker of relief in her expression.

"Fine." She yanks her phone from her pocket, dialing quickly. "There was a fire at High Five. Can my friend Aaron pick up Gabby? They won't let me leave."

I watch her as she talks, trying not to get distracted by her soft voice. She must be close to me in age. She's somewhere in her early thirties. Even covered in soot and frustration, she's gorgeous, making a white T-shirt and jeans look too good. And those freckles. Focus.

But I keep noticing every detail. The way her fingers tap against her leg. The little crease between her brows. She seems to handle stress well. Most people would be freaked out by a fire, but it's like it's not even phasing her. Where's her husband or family? Why is Aaron the one to help her out right now?

"Thank you, Aaron," she says, hanging up. "She's at Tot Academy."

Aaron nods. "Should I bring her here, or—?"

"How long until I can leave?" Claire asks, turning back to me with a pointed look.

"That's up to the paramedics."

She exhales sharply, muttering something under her breath that I don't catch.

"My key is under the planter next to my driveway," she says to Aaron. He nods, then turns and heads off.

As he disappears down the street, I continue to assess Claire. She's still sitting on the bumper, and the blanket hangs off one shoulder, forgotten. I should probably say something reassuring. Something that makes this easier.

Instead, I cross my arms. "You always this stubborn?"

She shoots me a sidelong look. "You always this annoying?"

I fight back a smirk. "Only when people put out a fire like it's no big deal."

Her lips twitch, like she's holding back a smile, and all I know is that I shouldn't be thinking about how much I want to see the full thing.

3

Claire

Annoyed, stressed, and aching—those are just a few words to describe how I feel. I'm in a daze as the paramedic asks me question after question, each one making my head throb more. I can barely focus. All I want to do is go home and cuddle with my little girl.

Moving to Wisconsin was supposed to be the fresh start Gabby and I both needed, but this moment reminds me how impossible it is to do everything on your own. You can't be everywhere at once. You can't do it all. Guilt creeps in as I think about Aaron rearranging his day for me while I'm stuck here, not with Gabby where I should be.

"All clear," the paramedic finally says, and I toss off the blanket. My sole focus is getting the hell out of here.

"You sure you want to drive?" the tall firefighter with too blue of eyes asks, his deep voice cutting through the fog of my thoughts.

I glance up at him. He's got that military rigidity about him, the way he stands with his back too straight. With his fire helmet off, I notice his shaggy blond hair. He is too tall and too buff. He's hot. That's just another annoyance right now. I don't have time for hot. I don't have time for any of this.

"They said all clear," I snap, already moving past him as fast as my legs will take me toward my car.

"You just put out a fire," his voice follows, steady and infuriating. "How about I drive you?"

"No," I bark, my fingers already gripping the door handle. *I need to get home to Gabby.*

Before I can open the door, he's right there, and with a firm push, he shuts it. The door slams closed, and my heart spikes—with anger and something else. His hand is too close to mine. His height and presence are imposing. I'm frozen, taken aback by him asserting himself.

"What the fuck?!" I stare up at him, eyes narrowing as I glare. He's standing too close now, his tall frame making me feel small, which only pisses me off more.

"Let me drive you." There's something almost gentle in his tone, but I can't focus on that. "I wouldn't feel right if you got behind the wheel."

"How would you drive in that?" I snap, looking at his fire suit, trying to break the moment, to break whatever weird tension is building between us.

"Don't worry about me." A soft smile grows as he steps closer. "Let's get you home."

The exhaustion hits me. Part of me wants to give in, to let him drive me home. But no. I've done everything on my own for so long, and I can't—won't—start letting someone else take over now. Especially not someone like him, someone so sure of himself.

"No," I say again, though the edge in my voice is softer this time. I reach for the door handle, but his hand doesn't move.

"It seems like you're used to handling things on your

own," he says, moving his hand back to his side. "But let me help you. You've been through enough today."

I pause. Even if he's right, I shake it off.

"I'll be fine." *I have to be fine.* I don't have any other option.

He doesn't say anything, just stands there, watching me. The firefighter is distracting in a way I don't want to admit.

"You're so stubborn," he says, but there's a hint of amusement in his tone.

"You have no idea."

Pulling the door open again, my heart is still racing from the way he's looking at me, the way he's *too* close.

Silently, I slide into my car, turning it on, refusing to make eye contact with him. I need to get to Gabby.

⭐
⭐
⭐

I step inside my home, a small, rented ranch-style place, closing the door quietly behind me. The smell of smoke is following me, embedded into my clothes. A reminder of the chaos from today. Everything from the fire, the panic, the noise—it's hard to shake off. My hands are still trembling a little. Despite trying to play it like I wasn't bothered by what happened, I want nothing more than to crawl into bed with Gabby and forget this day ever happened. I especially want to forget that I wasn't able to pick her up when she was sick.

Dropping my keys into the bowl, I see Gabby asleep on Aaron's chest. Her brown hair is pushed to one side, and she's in the same T-shirt dress and legging shorts from this morning.

At least she didn't have a big spill today.

I look around the place, suddenly embarrassed about the clutter. Toys fill the living room floor, and some papers are piled on the kitchen counter, otherwise nothing too embarrassing. I would have tidied up if I knew someone was coming over.

I approach them slowly, not wanting to wake her.

"Let me check her temperature," I whisper, seeing Gabby's flushed face. Walking down the hall to her room, I grab the ear thermometer from the basket on her dresser. Her room is the only one that's decorated. She wanted a forest theme, and we went all out with a gigantic tree wall sticker and a canopy over the chair in her reading corner. I smile, thinking back to doing this project with her, but then my mind races with what-if scenarios as I walk back to the living room. Delicately putting the thermometer in her ear, the number flashes after a few seconds. It's still a fever, but a low one. Four years into motherhood, you'd think I'd have a thicker skin by now, but every time she's sick, I'm a wreck.

I want to pick her up and hold her close. I want to feel her heartbeat against mine. But I smell like smoke and chemicals, and those toxins are absolutely not touching her.

"Go shower," Aaron whispers, reading my mind.

I open my mouth to protest, but he chuckles.

"We're comfortable here," he says, looking down at Gabby. I'm grateful for Aaron. Since meeting him in January when I applied to work at High Five, he's been nothing but nice and become the brother I never had.

"You don't need to be nap-trapped. Could you put her down in her bed? Then you can get on with your evening."

Aaron shifts carefully, his hand cradling Gabby's head. She looks so small in his arms compared to when I carry her. He effortlessly stands with all thirty-nine pounds of her; I'm jealous. I usually groan when I stand with her in my arms.

12

"Want me to tell Sarah how good you are with Gabby?" I tease, trying to lighten the mood.

Aaron smiles. "She already has baby fever," he whispers. "Keeps talking about how she'd turn one of the rooms in my house into a nursery and what she'd paint on the walls."

"Well ..." I nudge him with my elbow. "Wife her up and give her a baby, then."

"In time," he says with a wink. *They would have the cutest kids, brunette with big eyes.* Then Aaron's expression changes. "Are you okay? Do you need anything?"

"I'm good. I just need a shower."

Aaron disappears down the hall with Gabby, and I barely make it into the bathroom before the tears begin to well. Stripping off my clothes, I want to throw them away. I don't ever want to be reminded of this day. Everything that's happened hits me, and the tears fall.

I wasn't there for Gabby. I wasn't the one caring for her when she needed me. I was at the bar, fighting a fire.

Under the water, I fall apart. The hot stream washes away the grime, the smoke, whatever chemicals came out of the fire extinguisher—and I let myself sob. Hopefully Aaron is already gone. Hopefully no one can hear, but I can't hold back my emotions anymore.

I don't know how long I stand there, crying, but eventually, the water starts to calm me. I audibly exhale, feeling lighter with every loud breath.

"You got this," I encourage myself.

After I dry off, I peek in on Gabby. She's sound asleep in her toddler bed. We'll likely both be up in the middle of the night with her going to bed so early. She didn't have dinner. When was the last time she went to the bathroom? Should I wake her or let her keep sleeping?

I'll let her sleep.

Carefully, I shut her door. The house is silent. Aaron must be gone. In my towel, I confirm, looking around the house, and he is nowhere to be found. I'll have to get him a little something to thank him for all of his help today, I think, pacing to my room to get dressed.

Holding a pair of sweatpants, I hesitate. My thoughts wander back to the firefighter. Replaying the scene, I wish I wasn't thinking about how good looking he was. There were others there, but I didn't notice them. Who knew hot firefighters were real outside of TikTok? Especially in a town as small as this one. But the way he slammed my door, the way he commanded everything ... it made my heart race in a way it hasn't in a while.

I can manage five minutes of self-care right now. *Orgasms are nature's Ambian, right?*

Grabbing my toy, I slide under the covers, still naked, and think back to his commanding presence, his blue eyes, how fucking hot he looked in his fire suit. It's been months since a man's touched me. I push out how depressing that is and refocus on my new kink—firefighters. I'm about to press the setting to a higher intensity, but something else buzzes, and I groan. It's my phone.

Looking over, I see Nicholas O'Malley, the owner of High Five, is calling. I turn off my toy.

I have to take this.

"Hey," I answer, trying to sound chipper and normal but just sound frazzled.

"Claire, are you okay?" Nicholas asks, his voice full of concern. "Thank you for jumping into action. I'm so grateful."

"I'm fine," I say, shifting under the covers to sit. "It's no problem."

"I was thinking, how about you take the rest of the week off?"

"No way! The bar is going to be slammed for the holiday. You need—"

"I'm serious," Nicholas says, cutting me off.

"I need the money," I say softly. *Life's expensive.*

"How about I give you two thousand dollars to cover your shifts?"

"What?" My mouth drops open in disbelief. "No. That's too much."

"My bar could have burned down. Please, Claire. Enjoy the week off."

Two thousand dollars. That's more than I'd make with my scheduled shifts. It's more than my stretch goal. A lump forms in my throat as I try to respond.

"Thank you," I whisper. "Gabby's going to be excited to spend all day with me tomorrow."

"Aaron said she's sick. Do you need anything? I can make a run to the store for you."

"Nicholas, stop being so nice to all the single moms," I joke, trying to lighten the mood. *Emily Brown is lucky to have a guy like Nicholas.* All the moms need a guy like him, someone so caring and nice. The two of them have been unofficially campaigning for cutest couple in town since they started dating earlier this year. "We're good."

"If you need anything, call me, Aaron—any of us."

I smile, appreciating my work-family. "Thank you, seriously."

"Thank *you*. Seriously." Nicholas chuckles before hanging up.

I stare at my phone, still in shock. Two thousand dollars and a week off. Today is no longer the worst day ever.

4

Jake

E ntering High Five for happy hour, I set the gift bag on the wood bar, the cuddly brown teddy bear's ear peeking out from the top. This gesture can be read a lot of ways, but I haven't stopped thinking about Claire since she drove off yesterday. *What a first impression,* but I learned so much. She's a gorgeous, strong, caring mom who handles chaos better than half the Marines I know.

I keep replaying every moment we shared, searching for any hint of interest on her part. Even if she's not interested, part of me thinks she could've read our interaction as me being an insensitive asshole. But I couldn't let her leave before she was evaluated. I hope she understands that. Another part of me hopes she doesn't think I'm just another guy with a savior complex. *What if I've already blown it?*

Aaron, the manager, gives me a nod, approaching in a T-shirt and shorts. "Jake. What can I get you?"

"A beer. Something light in a bottle." I try to look casual as I search the crowded bar, but Claire's nowhere in sight.

The only indications of yesterday's fire are a closed sign in front of the women's bathroom and a newly printed all-gender bathroom sign covering the men's. Aaron pops the top off my beer and slides it across the bar.

"Is Claire here?" I ask, my eyes still drifting around the place. *Nicholas and Aaron did a great job refinishing all the wood in here a few months ago.*

Aaron raises an eyebrow, his gaze shifting to the gift bag. "She's not working today. We gave her the week off." He looks back to me, then at the bag again. "What's in the bag?"

"A little something for her and her daughter." I shrug, but I can feel my neck heating up, and tug at the collar of my polo. *This was probably a bad idea.*

Aaron lets out a short laugh. "Dude, you're not the first guy to fall for Claire Moore." He pauses, shaking his head. "She's happily single after her nasty divorce last year."

The word "single" makes me too excited, even though I'd assumed it. The way she carried herself yesterday makes more sense—strong but guarded, like she's used to relying on herself.

"I've never seen her around." I sip my beer, trying to cool down from the nerves I was just feeling.

"She moved here in January from Chicago. Lake Geneva is a clean slate for her and her daughter." Aaron studies me for a moment, squinting like he's trying to read my thoughts. "So, what are your intentions with her?" he asks, clearly enjoying himself.

I lift the bottle for another sip before answering. "To get her number. To take her out."

Aaron bites his lip. "She could use a night out ... you know what ... I'm feeling nice today. Let me text her that you're looking for her."

I watch as Aaron pulls out his phone, and my heart rate

picks up. He types the message, reading it aloud as he goes. "Jake, the firefighter from yesterday, is looking for you. He has a gift for you and Gabby in hand. What should I do?"

As Aaron sends the text, I try to act casual, but my foot taps against the stool leg.

Claire's been through a rough patch—marriage, divorce, raising a kid on her own—and here I am, thirty-four, no kids, and never married. I'd be lying if I said I haven't thought about settling down, finding someone. It just hasn't happened yet, and I'd like it to. I feel like I've gone out on a first date with everyone interesting in a twenty-mile radius of here. Well, everyone except Claire it seems.

"Let's see what she has to say." Aaron steps away, toward other patrons.

I take another sip of my beer, nearly in a sweat waiting to see how she responds.

5

Claire

Snuggling Gabby on the couch, I press my cheek against her warm forehead, grateful I get to spend the whole day comforting her. It's been forever since we've had a lazy day in the house. We hardly spend any time here, and it shows. The walls around us are bare. Watching her favorite cartoon, I feel relaxed until my mind drifts to the idea of texting her dad. Should I let him know she's sick? No. This is day two of this low-grade fever, and outside of her being a little lethargic, she seems good. She'll be recovered or at least a lot better by the time he picks her up tomorrow evening. There's no point in giving him an excuse to bail on his every-other-weekend duty. When he's with her, he's great—he loves to read Gabby stories and be outside with her. But getting him to show up is the hardest part. He's been able to come up with more than a few excuses about why he can't make the less than two-hour drive from Chicago or even the one-hour drive if we meet in the middle.

A familiar bitterness creeps in. My relaxation is over, and frustration takes hold. I'm the one who has to make up for his absences, who has to smooth over Gabby's disappointment when he can't make it. He acts like I should be so grateful for "his" money, like that makes up for everything or like it's even enough. But I would trade every cent for a dad who's consistent, who's a real presence in her life. A dad she sees more than the few days a month that he can barely manage.

My phone buzzes on the coffee table. Is this him canceling already? That would be like clockwork. Reaching for my phone, I see it's a text from Aaron. Do they need me at the bar? Are they already slammed?

AARON OLSON

> Jake, the firefighter from yesterday, is looking for you. He has a gift for you and Gabby in hand. What should I do?

Jake the firefighter.

A gift? For me and Gabby? Why am I smiling? I shake my head, almost laughing at myself. What a whiplash from being pre-mad at my ex to having some guy trying to be too cute. To have a guy trying, I repeat internally more than a few times. It's been a while since anyone has. Points for Jake.

At least he isn't a barfly. I've never seen him at High Five before, and I feel like I've met the whole town at this point since working there. More points for Jake.

But who is he? What does he want?

I glance down at Gabby, who's completely enthralled with her cartoon. We're both still in our pajamas and rocking bedhead, leaning into the lazy day. Maybe I should ignore this text, avoid the whole thing altogether. Curiosity gets the better of me though, and I type back a quick response.

CLAIRE MOORE

Do you know anything about this guy?

There's a long pause, and I imagine Aaron debating what to say. Then my phone buzzes again.

AARON OLSON

Good guy. Spent four years in the Marines after high school and is now a firefighter. Not a player.

I knew he was in the military! It was all over him. *Not a player.* I can't help but roll my eyes. If I had a dollar for every time someone vouched for a guy who turned out to be exactly what they swore he wasn't ... but Aaron wouldn't say it if it wasn't true.

CLAIRE MOORE

Are you trying to set me up?

AARON OLSON

Do you want to be set up?

What a question. *Do I?* I look down at Gabby's sweet, flushed face. I've gotten so used to keeping my guard up, to being cautious. Since the divorce, I've made sure she hasn't met anyone I've gone on a date with, not that there have been many. I went on one date that ended faster than it started and a few dates with another guy.

The flutter in my chest is saying I should let Aaron set me up. I mean, Jake's smokin' hot at the very least.

CLAIRE MOORE

Maybe.

Gabby stirs, snuggling closer, and I kiss the top of her

head. Whatever happens, I remind myself, I'll take it one step at a time. I've learned the hard way not to jump into things without thinking them through.

My phone buzzes again, and I glance at Aaron's reply, feeling that flutter in my chest grow a little stronger.

AARON OLSON

I'll let him know you're not uninterested. No pressure, though.

No pressure. I shake my head, realizing how I'm mindlessly smiling at my phone. Let's see what happens.

6

Jake

I lean forward on the bar, waiting for Aaron to share Claire's response. My fingers tap against the beer bottle nervously. When Aaron finally glances up from his phone, he chuckles softly.

"How about this," Aaron says while taking out a roll of receipt paper and tearing off a blank strip. He slides it across the bar toward me, along with a pen. "Write her a note about the date you want to take her on, along with your number, and I'll drop this gift off at her house after work."

"So, she's interested?"

"Maybe. She didn't say no, let's put it that way."

The tension in my chest loosens as I pick up the pen, flipping it between my fingers. This is a lot of pressure. I blankly stare at the receipt paper, thinking. A note. A date idea. I want to sound confident but not desperate.

I start scribbling a few words, but then scratch them out, crumpling the strip. "This is harder than I thought." Aaron hands me another strip of paper, and I take a sip of beer. What should I say? Finally, I decide to write from the heart, keeping it short:

Claire,

I find stubbornness very cute. I also think you're very cute. If you'd like to get dinner sometime, know I'm a complete gentleman. I'll pick you up, pay for dinner and the babysitter, and ensure you have a great time.

Biting my lip, I toy with writing the next sentence that popped in my head. Would it be too flirty to say that I like to spoil women? *Yeah.* Too flirty for where we are right now.

Here's my number, if you would like to take me up on this date.

I add my phone number at the bottom, then slide the note back over to Aaron. He glances at it, then nods, approving.

"Think she'll go for it?" *I want her to.*

Aaron tucks the note into the gift bag. "Only one way to find out, right?"

I nod, picking up my beer and taking a long sip. I'm not afraid to put myself out there, but this note … it's more vulnerable than I've been in a while.

As Aaron claps a hand on my shoulder and heads off to help some new customers, I'm left alone with my thoughts, imagining what it would be like if she says yes. I picture the two of us at a quiet corner table in a restaurant. I didn't see her smile once yesterday. I'd love to see her smile and watch the stress fade from her face. I want to make her laugh and show her how special she is.

7

Claire

Thursday, July 3rd

Reading the note for maybe the twentieth time, I don't know what to do. Sleeping on it didn't help either. Do I go out with the firefighter? I wish I didn't feel so skeptical.

Pay for the babysitter? Maybe he has a single mom kink. This is some experienced single-mom flirting.

Don't be so jaded. Nicholas could have coached him at the bar yesterday. It's really thoughtful to think about that. Little does he know I'm going to be child-free for a couple of nights.

I stare at the note, eating another truffle from the box of chocolates that were in the bag. My mind flashes to the dates I've been on since the divorce. One guy had an intense timeline for marriage and kids. Who knows if I'll ever do that again, marriage and more kids. Most days, I'm too overwhelmed to even remember to eat, let alone add more responsibility to my life.

Tonight, I'll be both child-free and not working. I can't

26

remember the last time the stars aligned like that. So, it's a choice between reading a book in the bathtub or a date with a hot firefighter. The safe option or the risky one.

I've never gone for a Captain-America-looking guy before. Blond hair, blue eyes, military, and named Jake. *How unoriginal.* Not that my red hair, blue eyes, girl named Claire, Chicago suburban, Irish self is all that original.

Jake's nothing like the guys I typically go for. For whatever reason, guys with accents have always been my weakness. Especially guys born outside of the States. My ex's voice always did make me melt—before everything fell apart, anyway.

What's the worst that could happen? The date sucks, and I leave. No harm done.

Marriage changed me. I used to be an eternal optimist. But now ... I'm more cautious. Maybe it's time to lower my defenses just a little. Just for tonight.

Fuck it. If he can take me out tonight, he gets a date. If he can't, then he won't.

CLAIRE MOORE

> Thank you for the chocolates and stuffed animal. It was very sweet. You can take me out to dinner tonight.

I giggle when I see how fast I get a response.

JAKE THE FIREFIGHTER

> Tonight. Perfect. I'd like to pick you up at seven and take you to La Nonna.

Now *that's* a first date. The most expensive restaurant in town. On a holiday weekend ... there's no way we can get a table.

CLAIRE MOORE

You sure you can get a reservation on such short notice?

JAKE THE FIREFIGHTER

Positive. If you want to do that, we'll do that. We can go anywhere you want, but I'm hoping you let me take you to the nicest place in town.

Stop smiling! Although this is sounding more exciting than my book and bath by the minute.

CLAIRE MOORE

La Nonna it is. And no babysitter necessary. My daughter will be with her dad for the weekend.

Please don't cancel at the last minute, I beg the universe. But I doubt he'd miss the chance to parade her around like a trophy at his brother-in-law's lake house nearby on Delavan Lake. He'll have a full weekend of everyone telling him how great of a father he is and how much of a bitch I am for leaving Chicago and petitioning for primary custody.

It's fine. In this small town, she can have a normal childhood where preschool isn't tens of thousands of dollars and where you can walk on the sidewalk without having to look over your shoulder. It's what's best for her, and it's also what's best for me. There was no reason for me to stay in the city once we were done. Honestly, I don't know where we'll be in five years, but Lake Geneva is good for now.

My phone buzzes with a call from Jake, surprising me. *Wait. Why is Jake calling me?* I look at Gabby playing with her new stuffed animal on the living room floor and make my way to the kitchen.

"Hi," I answer, sounding more nervous than I'd like.

28

"Hey. How are you doing after yesterday?" His voice is sexier than I remember, and it's messing with me.

"Fine."

"It's okay to say the fire was scary."

"It was scary." I giggle, surprising myself with that noise.

"I'm really looking forward to tonight."

"Is this, like, your thing ... picking up girls you meet on the scene?"

He chuckles. "There's never been anyone as beautiful as you." I roll my eyes, but a smile tugs at my lips. "That's not a line," he says into the silence. "Is seven good, or what time do you want me to pick you up?"

"Wouldn't table availability dictate that?"

"There are perks to my job. The owners of La Nonna treat me like a king ever since we put out a kitchen fire a while back. If I call them, they'll give us a table whenever we want."

I guess he always makes friends on the scene then. It's cute. "Let's do six. I'm an early bird."

"Six. I can't wait to see you in a less stressful environment."

I'm smiling too much in agreement. "See you there."

"There? No. Let me pick you up. Text me your address."

"Okay," I relent with no sass. I should have put up more of a protest there, but whatever. *Captain America* is picking me up now. He probably drives a truck and will be wearing cowboy boots. I really hope neither are true.

I hang up after giving him my address and saying our goodbyes. Opening the fridge, I blankly stare at it. *What am I doing*, getting excited about a date with a guy who probably has toxic masculinity seeping from his pores? A military guy who's now a firefighter, a far cry from the entrepreneurs and WASPy finance guys I usually go for. Not that those guys have worked out well for me. I shouldn't judge Jake so hard. My gut doesn't get bad vibes. *Lower the guard,* I remind myself.

⭐
⭐
⭐

Looking at my phone, it's almost time for my ex to pick up Gabby. I try to push aside the anxiety that always builds as his arrival gets closer. After checking for the fourth time that she has everything she needs, I feel confident I didn't forget to pack anything.

"Lista?" I ask, looking down at her. Her dad is only a couple of minutes away.

"Si, mama," she says, excited. She's always excited to see her dad. I don't want to put my feelings toward him on her.

"Bueno."

My ex isn't the worst human on the planet. Every time I speak Spanish, I think about the early days of our relationship. Him wooing me. I'd never met someone from Argentina before. He was so smooth, so captivating.

But he can't keep it in his fucking pants. At first, I brushed it off—cultural differences, monogamy is a patriarchal concept anyways. I mean our marriage was never traditional. It was open. It was easier to be open than constantly fight about his girls on the side. But when he was actively choosing his then girlfriend over me and this baby he begged for ... that's not what we agreed to. Gabby and I were supposed to be his top priorities. It still makes me mad that I was second fucking fiddle in my own home. He's a self-centered prick. Always has been. Always will be.

"Claire," he says in a voice I wish I didn't find attractive with a face I want to punch as he stands on my doorstep.

"Samuel," I greet tightly, noting how his brown hair has more gray since the last time I saw him. "Remember, if she eats past seven, she will have nightmares. I know your family eats late, but this is a proven thing. Don't let your mom tell you it's all in my head. If you want to sleep for the next couple of nights, do not feed her late."

"Relájate."

"Don't tell me to relax." I squint at him, then bend down to hug Gabby. "I miss you already. Have so much fun swimming with your cousins."

"Bye, Mommy."

I squeeze her tight, grateful I only have to part with her a few days a month. Shutting the door, I stare blankly at my living room for a moment. *Free time.*

I lean into the silence. What am I going to do before my date? I have to shave my legs, that's for sure. Maybe I could organize ... *no.* I need to take this time to relax.

8

Jake

Starting my vintage blue Camaro, I'm too excited about this date. Driving across town to pick her up, I play some comfort music. There's something about blasting Kings of Leon while driving this car that makes me feel like I'm in a movie.

Cutting the engine, I'm suddenly more nervous than I thought I would be, seeing Claire already outside. *Now that's a dress.* She looks incredible in a flowy, peach sundress with cutouts at the waist. Sliding out of my car, she smiles as I approach her modest home. Her smile. *Shit.* It's beautiful. Absolutely gorgeous. Claire is breathtaking. I want to go in for a hug, but we're strangers. I hesitate, standing in front of her.

"You look nice," she says before I can think of something to say. There's a hint of surprise in her tone, as if she wasn't expecting me to clean up well. I guess she only saw me in my fire suit. Claire has no idea what my style would be. Not that I have *style*. But my mom enforced the idea that you need to look good when you leave the house.

"You look better." *Fuck.* I don't want that to sound weird like she looks better than she did yesterday. Of course, she looks better than yesterday. "I mean, you look better than me."

"Thank you. White's an interesting choice for tonight." She teases, checking me out.

"You think I don't know how to use a fork and knife?" I joke, looking down at my white linen polo, khaki shorts, and brand-new white tennis shoes.

She laughs lightly, then looks over at the Camaro. "Cool car."

"Don't sound so surprised about everything. It's hurting my ego."

Her smile grows devilish. *I like this girl.* We walk a few steps until I open the car door for her.

"I assumed you would pick me up in a truck," she says, sliding in.

"Maybe next time."

"Of course, you have a truck."

I'm smiling too much, walking to my side of the car. *She's feisty,* and I love that. "What's that supposed to mean?" I ask, buckling myself in and looking over at her. She brushes her red hair to one side. It's beautiful.

"You're the target market for a truck," she quips before glancing around the car, running a hand over the leather. "Bench seat. What year is this?"

"Sixty-seven. Are you into cars?" I ask, surprised.

"My dad was really into cars."

"*Was?*"

"He died a few years ago. Cancer," she says, matter-of-fact.

I squeeze her hand. "I'm sorry to hear that."

"Just know that if you have sloppy shifts, he's judging you."

Smirking, I start the engine and the car rumbles beneath us.

"Now I'm focused on my shifts instead of you." I wink.

Pulling away from the curb, we'll arrive at La Nonna in less than five minutes. I steal glances at her, breaking my eye contact from the road. The way she carries herself. The way she's comfortable in silence. This woman has layers. I can't wait to get to know more about her over dinner.

"Did you restore it?" Claire asks, breaking the silence.

"No. I got it at an estate sale a couple of years ago."

I shouldn't be surprised to see all of the parking spaces filled as we drive down Main Street. In Lake Geneva, it feels like the town's population increases tenfold on weekends, especially holidays.

"Holiday weekends," I mutter.

"FIBs am I right?" She softly laughs.

I haven't heard that expression in a while. *Fucking Illinois bastards.*

"Hey, didn't you used to be a FIB?" I tease, curious to learn more about her although I've been asking around.

"Born and raised," she clips.

"Switching allegiances?"

"Well, I did get a Wisconsin driver's license ..."

"You're a cheese head now."

"Looks that way," she says, smiling bright.

Finding an open spot, I pull in, flick the key, and look at Claire.

"Make sure you order too much food," I encourage, giving her hand a quick squeeze, then unbuckle my seatbelt. I don't want her to feel self-conscious about anything tonight.

"You want me to be an expensive date?" she asks teasingly.

I want to spoil her.

"I want you to get what you want." I smirk, getting out to open the door for her.

9

Claire

Jake pulls the chair out for me. *He's sweet.* I admire the restaurant while he takes his seat. I've never been here before. La Nonna. The fanciest restaurant in town. I've walked past it many times and am excited to finally eat here. It's cozy but elegant, with upscale finishes and white tablecloths.

"Hey Jake," a twenty-something blonde says, approaching the table, cutting through the humming chatter of the full restaurant.

"Anna. Nice to see you."

She smiles at me, and I recognize her. I've seen her in High Five before. "You work at High Five, right?" she asks after staring at me for a moment.

"Yeah. I'm Claire."

She glances between Jake and me. "Do you want to order some wine? Maybe a bottle of Chianti?"

Jake raises an eyebrow, leaving the decision to me. *What do I want?* I don't need to impress him by pretending to be a wine connoisseur.

"I'm more of a cocktail girl," I share, looking directly at him, then glancing back at the server. "I'll have a Negroni."

"Oh. I haven't had one of those in a while." He sounds genuinely excited. I don't know why, but that excitement makes me smile. "I'll have the same," he orders.

"Great ... and Jake, were you the one that pranked Chad's truck?"

"What?" he asks, sounding confused.

"Good. I'm happy it wasn't you. I figured it was another one of the lost boys that refuses to grow up."

"Don't lump me in with the guys." Jake laughs.

"You're friends with Chad. You're guilty by association," Anna chides and then says, "I'll give you a few minutes."

"You know her?" I ask, curious about that interaction.

"She's dating one of my best friends."

I shouldn't judge. I was that girl. The younger girl with the older guy. But part of me wants to tell her all of the red flags to look out for. I sip my water. "You're still pranking?"

"I was not involved in whatever she's talking about," he says with a shrug.

This date feels easy so far. It's going better than I anticipated.

"It's not that I don't like wine, by the way," I share, wanting to keep the conversation flowing after a growing pause. "But I prefer a cocktail. Also, I don't like to drink while I eat. I'm more of a pre- and post-meal cocktail person."

"I'm not much of a wine guy either." He leans back in his chair slightly. There's an easy charm to him, like he's used to being comfortable in his own skin. Maybe it's the confidence that comes with looking like *this*—strong, tall, and *too* good looking.

"So, you were going to suffer through for me?" I ask, raising an eyebrow, teasing him. A defense mechanism I am well aware of. The more I tease, the more interested I am in a guy.

He chuckles softly. "Nothing about this is suffering."

Both of our blue eyes are locked on each other. *Captain America is blistering hot.* It's effortless hotness even though there's effort in everything. The way his shaggy blond hair perfectly falls, the way his shirt fits just right. Annoyingly hot.

"I like that you don't have a buzz cut," I say with a little smirk. "Feeling rebellious after leaving the military?"

"Were you asking about me?"

"Aaron shared a couple things about you with me."

"Just a couple?"

I bite my lip, loving the way he is looking at me. He's barely broken eye contact since we've sat down, and the intensity behind his eyes, it's smoldering.

"After four years of being forced to have short hair, I'm good." He runs his hands through his hair. If he's trying to show off his biceps with that move, it's working. *Is that a tattoo peeking through the sleeve of his polo?* "Who knows when it will start falling out, so why not?"

He easily shrugs, and I need to steer my thoughts away from what could happen after dinner, so I ask, "What's the most embarrassing thing you've done in the last year?"

The confidence slips from his face for a moment, and that shouldn't make me smile. "Our department did a calendar fundraiser ... I was August."

I burst out laughing, imagining him shirtless, posing with a fire hose or something cheesy. "Show me!" I demand, extending my hand playfully.

He shakes his head. "No phones on dates."

"No phones on dates?" I mimic him.

"I like to stay present. There are too many distractions these days, and when I'm on a date, that's my sole focus."

He's genuine and sincere. *Why did I just bite my lip?* "What other rules do you have about dating?"

"I don't have more than two drinks on a date. And I always pay." He looks down at the table for a moment.

"What?"

"And, nothing more than a kiss on the first date."

"How very gentlemanly of you," I quip, resting my chin in my hand. I equally appreciate it and hate it. No sexy fire-fighter time tonight. Got it. But a part of me admires the restraint. Maybe he's different from the guys I've been with before—guys who rush into things without a second thought.

"It's just ... I like to take things slow."

Jake's lip bite. Am I blushing? *Where's my drink?* I'm definitely sweating.

"Take things slow?" I flirt back.

Anna sets the drink in front of me, and I flinch. I was wrapped up in that flirty fucking moment. I hate how attracted I am to this guy. I grab for my drink, staring down at it, needing to regain my composure.

"Ready to order?" Anna asks, blissfully unaware of the heated moment she just stepped into.

Jake gestures toward me.

"Gnocchi bolognese," I order.

"Pork chop milanese," Jake says, turning back to me with warm eyes. "What do you think about starting with carpaccio?" I nod. "And carpaccio, please."

He says both dishes correctly. *The plot thickens with Jake.* There's more to him than his looks. *I kind of wish he was just surface level and boring.* That's easier. But now,

I'm intrigued. Anna leaves, and I turn my attention back to him.

"Your pronunciation was impressive."

"Is that a compliment without any snark?" he asks, raising an eyebrow before sipping his drink.

"Snark?" I feign innocence.

"All of your compliments have had little digs in them so far."

I sip my Negroni, smiling back. "So, tell me ... *do* you have a thing for single moms?"

"Deflecting is a tell for you, in case you didn't know," he cooly says, tapping his glass with mine.

"You're smarter than I was anticipating," I tease, taking another sip of my drink, giving him that snark.

"Why do you think I'm smart?" he asks with a sly smile.

"Because you know how your acting works."

"I'm not acting."

"Time will tell."

"Acting hard to get is very sexy."

"I'm not acting."

"Time will tell." He chuckles, clearly amused with himself. But I'm amused too, laughing, smiling. "I go to High Five a couple of times a month. I'm surprised I've never seen you."

"I work weekday day shifts. On weekends, when my daughter is with her dad, I'll pick up a shift or two."

"I'm not much of a day drinker. Really, not that much of a drinker. Just here and there."

"Same."

"Carpaccio," Anna's voice breaks through.

"If you make a raw meat joke, you're losing some points," I tease, staring at the dish.

10

Jake

"You wish I was that simple," I tease back, stunned—*in the best way*—by how this date is going. Claire is fucking gorgeous, but there's more to her than looks. She's challenging me at every turn, and I'm loving it. There's something refreshing about a woman who doesn't hold back, who pushes and prods like she's testing what I'm made of.

"Do you want another one?" I ask, eyeing her empty drink.

"After we're done eating, yes." Then a sly smile grows on her face. "If you have one more drink, are you going to be more or less inclined to break your rules?"

I nearly grumble. *Is she teasing me, or does she seriously want to hook up?* "It wouldn't matter. Rules are rules."

"Another hard habit to shake from the military?"

"There are plenty of lingering habits from the military ... like waking up super early. The Marine discipline is drilled into me."

"So, you never break the rules?" she flirts.

"Who are we without our principles?" I say, leaning

forward. She smiles down at the food, avoiding my gaze, and I watch her cut her appetizer into small bites. "Are you hoping that with another drink, I'll objectify you?"

"Hoping?" she mocks, looking up through her lashes. She knows exactly what she's doing, and I'm here for it.

"If you want me to tell you that you're the sexiest fucking woman I've ever seen, I'll just tell you."

She bites her thumbnail, her blue eyes staring deeply into mine.

"If you want me to tell you that your action-figure aesthetic is working for you," she says, with a growing smile, "then I guess I will."

"Action figure." I chuckle. "If you're looking for a toy, then I don't think this is going to work."

"I'm not looking for anything," she shoots back, her tone more serious than I expected. Her words hang in the air between us.

I set my elbow on the table, resting my head in my hand, taking her in. "I don't believe you," I whisper, selfishly hoping the response is her defense mechanism and not the truth. Because I want more.

We eat silently for a moment, and I take the time to think. I've been on plenty of dates this year, but this one feels different. There's real potential here, but she's so guarded. Maybe she really isn't looking for something serious, or maybe she's afraid to admit she could be. I can't tell yet, but I want to find out.

"Tell me about your daughter," I say, shifting gears. "How's she doing? I kind of guessed a stuffed animal would be appropriate since you said she was at Tot Academy."

"She loves stuffed animals, so thank you," Claire says, and her expression softens. "Gabriella ... Gabby is feeling better. Minutes before the fire alarm went off, they called me saying she had a fever, so I was stressed about needing to pick her up. That's why I was frazzled."

"You handle pressure well," I say, watching her closely. "I wouldn't say you were frazzled. Stubborn for sure." I wink, trying to ease the tension.

"Well, I'm a redhead. I think by birthright I have to be."

And she's funny. I check Claire out, letting my eyes linger on her chest a moment longer than I have all night, then flick my eyes back to her face, captivated.

"How old is your daughter?" I ask, wanting to peel back the layers.

"She turned four a couple of months ago."

Four. Claire looks about my age, maybe a couple of years younger. It makes me admire how she's managed everything—the divorce, the move, being a single mom. She's one strong woman.

"When did you move to Wisconsin?" I ask, although I already know.

"In January. Once the divorce was final, and we had our custody agreement locked in," she says, her tone more guarded again.

"I'm curious, but I don't want to press." *It wouldn't be polite to grill her about this, although I want to know.*

"Maybe in a couple of dates we can get more into all of that," she says, and I nod, understanding.

More dates. I try not to smirk, excited about the idea of more dates. I don't need all the answers right now, but I'm already thinking ahead—our next date.

"So you want to go out with me again?"

Claire takes a bite of her gnocchi.

"Are you trying to get yourself some more time? Or just trying to make me nervous?" I tease.

She laughs, covering her mouth.

"I don't have that much free time."

"Aaron said something about you getting the week off."

"Did he?" I nod, and she smiles. "I'm free tomorrow, Saturday, and half of the day on Sunday."

"I work tomorrow night. The barge setting off fireworks could catch fire. I'll be manning the fireboat. How do you feel about a morning date?"

"You want to see me tomorrow morning?" Claire sounds too surprised.

"Yes."

She's smiling, but she isn't saying anything.

"No pressure," I add, trying to give her an easy out. "I'm sure you want to just chill by yourself too."

"I like walking on the lake path and haven't done it enough this summer. Want to go for a morning walk?"

"That sounds great. What's your coffee order?"

"Why?"

"When I pick you up, I'll bring coffee."

I want to bring her a morning treat before our long walk, the perfect date to keep peeling back her layers. I want to know everything about her.

11

Claire

I s *this guy for real?* I wonder as I look across the table at Jake. He's sweet and considerate ... almost too good to be true. *Who do I have to thank for him being this way?* His mom? His ex? It's hard to believe someone can be this good without a catch. *But there's always a catch.*

"A vanilla latte, no whipped cream," I say when he asks about my coffee order for tomorrow. He's already planning our morning date, and I'm letting myself get swept into it.

"What time should I pick you up? The sun rises around five thirty."

"You casually know when the sun rises?"

"A habit from the Marines," he explains. "I don't need an alarm. I'm up at zero dark thirty every day."

Of course, he's disciplined. Before Gabby, this fact would have been a red flag, but I'm also up early each day.

"Tomorrow is a rare opportunity for me to sleep in," I say with a small laugh, "but I'll be awake by seven, guaranteed."

Anna, our server, approaches the table. "Looks like we enjoyed everything. Would you like anything else? Boxes?"

Jake doesn't hesitate to ask, "You still want that post-meal cocktail?"

"I'd love one more negroni, thanks." It's been a long time since I felt this comfortable with someone.

"Same here," he adds, and Anna walks away.

"How about you pick me up at seven-thirty?"

"Roger that," Jake says, and the smile on his face ... *he's a Golden Retriever*, I think, shaking my head internally. He's just so ... happy. Where are the red flags? Where are the flaws? It's almost like he's *too* perfect.

"I feel like you're judging me," he says, tilting his head like he's catching onto my internal monologue.

"My internal thoughts are less skeptical about you than when this date started."

Jake reaches for my hand, squeezing it gently. His hand is big and strong. I glance down at our hands, loosely holding each other on the table. It's strange how natural this feels—*like this isn't our first date*, like we've known each other longer. I glance back up at him, smiling, enjoying this moment, and then down at our hands again. My mind briefly wanders to the last time I felt this at ease with someone. *It's been a while.*

"Tell me some more habits from the Marines that are hard to break." The Marines must have shaped him. Maybe if I understand more about him, I can find something that makes him less perfect—something more human.

"I have to work out every day."

"*Have* to?"

"I feel out of whack if I don't. Plus, at the station, there's a lot of downtime, so it's easy to fit it in."

"I go in waves with working out," I admit, unsure why I'm sharing this. "Currently, I'm not working out much."

"Don't be too hard on yourself. You're on your feet all day, and I'm sure you're picking up and carrying your daughter around. More activity than most."

It's sweet, but all I can think about is how jigglier I feel compared to where I want to be. Especially compared to his perfect *fucking* body. I glance down at the table, tempted to deflect, to brush it off.

"You look great. Don't stress about it."

"Can you read my mind?" I joke, but there's a nervousness in my voice. I don't think I'm that easy of a book to read.

"I'm learning your face."

Before I can respond, Anna returns, sliding our cocktails in front of us. The timing couldn't be better, a distraction from this feeling of vulnerability.

He holds his glass up for a toast. "To learning how to read each other."

I lift my glass, clinking it against his. But I'm less present, getting lost in my thoughts.

Learning to read each other. That's what I'm doing, isn't it? Trying to figure out if this is real. Trying to figure out if I can trust him. If I can trust myself again. *I don't want to get hurt.* Most of all, I don't want to be let down again.

As we sip our drinks, I try to push all those thoughts out and enjoy this great date. *But that nagging voice is still there.* It's always there.

"Do you have any siblings?" I ask. Maybe learning more about Jake will help me get out of my head. "Tell me about your family."

"I have an older brother and a younger sister. Neither of them live in the Midwest anymore. My parents live a couple of towns over, and we're pretty close. Like Saturday night dinners together, and I help them around the house when stuff breaks."

Of course, he has a close family. *Of course, he's the perfect guy who helps his parents.* I shouldn't internally groan, but I do. He keeps getting more and more perfect, and I'm waiting for the flaw that never shows up. I feel like I'm a few sentences away from giving in, from letting myself believe this is real.

"What about you?" he asks after I awkwardly don't respond right away.

"As I mentioned, my dad passed. My mom is toxic." I make a scrunch face and then sip my drink. "I cut her out of my life in my twenties. Gabby hasn't met her ... I feel guilty about it sometimes, but I know it's for the best."

Jake squeezes my hand again. If we keep going out on dates, I'll have to talk about all this shit ... my mom, my ex. *Agh!* I hate talking about these things.

"My younger sister lives in Phoenix," I add, refocusing. "We see each other a couple of times a year. We're close but not, like, best friends."

"So, you're really doing it alone up here?"

"Yeah."

"Why move here?"

I shake my head, not wanting to dive into all of that tonight. "Too long of a story."

"What's the abbreviated version?"

"I've always liked visiting this area. It's close enough yet far enough away from Chicago, where Gabby's dad lives. It feels like a fresh start."

"You think you'll stick around?"

"Why?"

"Long distance sucks."

I laugh, but I hold back from shutting down the flirtation.

Jake eyes my empty drink. "Should I get you back?"

I nod, thinking about how I like living in Wisconsin, but I don't know what the future holds for Gabby and me.

12

Jake

Claire and I keep stealing quick glances at each other as we walk out of the restaurant. I love July evenings, the residual warmth from the day. I go for her hand, holding it as we stroll down Main Street. This date was amazing, and I'm already looking forward to seeing her tomorrow morning. Something is building between us, something bigger than a casual date.

"Want to drive?" I ask, looking down at her.

"What?" she asks, sounding surprised.

"Let's see how sloppy your shifts are," I tease, nudging her lightly.

"That's a lot of trust for a girl you just met."

"I get a good feeling you won't crash or burn my clutch."

She squints at me, then sticks out her hand. "I'm really out of practice."

"Get back in the game, then." I hand over the keys. A small part of me is excited to see how she handles it. There's something incredibly sexy about her confidence.

"I'm guessing this seat doesn't move forward," she says, slipping into the driver's seat.

"It's welded into place." Claire scootches close to the edge of the seat to reach the pedals. She starts the car, the low rumble of the engine filling the air. "Go down a back road. Let's joyride for a bit."

I don't want this night to end. Watching her drive, my eyes drift to the cutouts in her dress and the exposed skin. *Just a kiss goodnight,* I remind myself. The rest will have to wait.

"This car sounds so sexy," Claire says, looking my way.

That smile, those eyes—she's letting go, and it's the most carefree I've seen her tonight. Carefree is a really good look for her.

Driving out of town, heading toward a back country road, she accelerates hard, and we both burst into laughter after our heads are tossed back. Enjoying the thrill together, there's a freedom in this moment. It's just the two of us enjoying the quiet roads.

"I like this car."

"Drive faster." I don't want her to hold back. I want her to keep leaning into the excitement.

She raises an eyebrow at me before she presses down on the gas, shifting smoothly as the cornfields blur by. *This is summer,* the endless evening light, the road stretching ahead of us. I can't stop admiring her—*Claire has skills.*

"Should I turn on some music?" I ask, because I love blasting music in this car.

"As long as it's not country, we're good."

"What do you have against country music?" I ask, narrowing my eyes.

Claire looks over, raising a sassy brow, then looks back at the road. I guess that's her answer and I smirk, turning on The Black Keys. It seems like the right vibe for this moment.

At a stop sign, she glances at me, mischief written all over her face. "Shall I drag start?"

I laugh, impressed with her boldness. "A new clutch is worth it if this goes bad. Let's see what you've got."

She revs the engine, the car growling beneath us, and then accelerates, shifting fast as we take off. *Impressive.* "Were you a bank robber at some point?" I tease, wondering how she is so good at this.

Claire laughs softly, slowing down as we head back toward Lake Geneva. "That was fun. I haven't driven like that in a long time."

"You're very sexy driving this car." It's not just the driving that's hooking me—it's everything about her. The way she handles herself, the way she laughs, the way she challenges me. *And how fucking sexy she is.*

She smiles, but she doesn't look at me. I reach out, resting my hand on her thigh, giving it a small squeeze. *I'm falling for her, I know that much.* "I'm really looking forward to seeing you tomorrow morning."

"Thank you for being interesting," she says, looking over at me, and there's a softness in her voice. She's lowering her guard.

We drive in comfortable silence for a minute. Maybe we're both thinking about how well this is going?

When she parks on the curb, we're staring at each other. The air feels thick with tension, the kind that's been building all night. *I want to kiss her,* but I don't want to assume. I should ask, but I'm hesitating. My eyes dart between her lips and her eyes, trying to decide my next move.

"Kiss me already," she whispers.

I lean in, cupping her face gently in my hand. The moment our lips meet, I know my life's changed. The energy. The electricity. My body is on fire just from the touch of her lips. As I slide my tongue into her mouth, Claire straddles me, her arms wrapping around my neck. I haven't had a car make-out like this in years, and it feels like we're both teenagers again, lost in the heat of the moment. My hands explore the bare skin on her ribs through the cutouts before trailing down the back of her dress. Our kisses become more feverish, more desperate. Claire's hands run down my chest. Her fingers are teasing, barely dipping below my jeans, pressing into my hip bones.

"Are you testing me?" I lean back, chuckling softly, trying to regain some control.

"What?"

That tone. She's feigning innocence.

"I'm a man of my word."

She leans in teasingly close to my lips. "We're just making out." We stare at each other, and a bratty smile is growing on her face. "This might be a first." She laughs, as I keep my hands at my sides, off of her body. "A guy pumping the brakes."

I exhale loudly, leaning my head against the bench seat, trying to calm myself down. She has me so turned on I can barely think straight. But I don't want to ruin this by rushing. "Why are you playing games?" I ask, the frustration evident in my tone.

Her brows furrow. "What?"

"You know kissing is all that's on the table tonight. Why are you trying to do more?"

She shifts, crossing her arms but looking away, a flicker of guilt or maybe defensiveness in her expression. "I didn't know how much that rule was telling people what they want to hear versus the truth."

"I'm straightforward."

"Okay," she says quietly, almost like she's unsure if she believes me. Her eyes drop to her lap, and her shoulders sink a little—deflated.

"If you want to know if I want more, of course I do, but we have plenty of time to get there as we keep dating."

"Dating?" she repeats, her voice rising in surprise.

"Yeah," I say, smiling. "Next date starts in less than twelve hours." I wink.

"So, what's the most that can happen on the next date?"

I grumble, both appreciating and hating how she's pushing me. "This is how it's going to be, huh?" She sassily raises her eyebrows, signaling for me to continue. "I'm very disciplined. I know how to be uncomfortable. Don't think your feminine wiles can sway that."

Claire rolls her eyes, but I can see the smile she's desperately trying to hold back. I pull her in for another kiss. "Let me treat you right." There's a pause between us before she slides off my lap. "What are you thinking about?"

"I think you're looking for something serious, and I don't know what I'm looking for."

"More reason for us not to rush anything." I squeeze her thigh gently. I want to take my time with this, with her, because I am looking for something serious.

She smirks, her eyes flicking to the door handle. "Do you expect me to open this myself?"

I chuckle, getting out of the car and walking around to open her door. I reach for her hand, interlacing our fingers as we walk to her front stoop. "Your vanilla latte, no whipped cream, will arrive at seven-thirty tomorrow," I remind her.

"This was really fun. Thank you."

"More fun tomorrow," I say, leaning in to kiss her one last time.

"More fun inside?" she tests, squeezing my hand.

"Claire ..." *Is she playing games or is she testing me?* Or both?

"I rarely have the place to myself."

I press her against the door, staring deeply into her eyes. Turned on, I'm nearing my wits end and considering breaking the rules. Of course I want her, but it's too soon. "You can have more fun inside, but we're done having fun tonight."

She squints at me.

"You're going inside, locking your door, and grabbing a toy."

"A toy?" She blinks, surprised.

"You know what I'm talking about." I trail my hand up her thigh. "Lay in bed and think about what you want me to do to you ..." Claire bites her lip. "After you come, text me that the mission is complete, and then go to bed."

Her chest rises, deeply inhaling. Maybe she's wondering how serious I am. "I better get that text before I get home too."

"Why would I do that?"

I press a firm kiss to her lips. "No dilly dallying." I trace her lips with my fingers. "Go inside and get to work."

She bites her lip, turning to her door. I swat her lightly on the ass when she opens it, and her head immediately turns back.

She squints playfully before saying, "I'm relieved you're not boring in this way." Claire steps into the house, and I hear the lock flip behind her. Walking back to the car, I'm smiling to myself. *What a night.*

I drive home in silence, replaying our date, curious if she'll complete the mission. I'm more than a little distracted thinking about her and what she could be doing right now.

But I can also see her wanting to be defiant. Not wanting to give me this since I didn't go inside. *How much of a brat is she?* I'm still nervous about where she's at emotionally. But I want more than sex from Claire. I want everything she's willing to give me.

Pressing the garage door button, my phone lights up with a new text.

CLAIRE MOORE

Mission complete.

Staring at my phone, the shit eating grin on my face says it all. She's fucking perfect.

JAKE SCHMIDT

Good girl.

13

Claire

Friday, July 4th

I chuckle at how prompt Jake is, parking his red truck on the curb exactly at seven-thirty. *Of course, he drives a big red pickup truck*, I think, stepping out of my house and locking the door behind me.

A smile grows as I think about last night's mission. There's an excitement bubbling inside me for this low-pressure date. As I approach, I check him out in an army-green Marine's shirt and black shorts.

"I wasn't expecting your shorts to be shorter than mine," I tease, trying to keep things light despite the butterflies. I can't believe he told me to get off with a toy last night, and that I did it.

Good girl. I was not expecting him to be like that. But I guess with the military, it tracks?

He laughs deeply. "At least yours are tighter." I look down at my bike shorts and a baggy shirt. "Where's my coffee?"

"In the truck," he says, grabbing my hand and easing me

57

toward him. We share a sweet kiss until he tugs on my ponytail.

I pull back slightly, smiling entirely too much. "Why'd you do that?"

"I love ponytails."

Jake. His flirtation feels easy, effortless.

With our fingers interlaced, we walk toward the truck, but my smile fades when I notice something in the back window—a black American flag with a red stripe window cling. A Red Lives Matter sticker. *There it is—the red flag I was looking for.* A fucking literal red flag.

I pause, awkwardly standing outside the truck when he opens the door. The sight of that sticker makes me go back to my immediate assumption. He was in the military. He's a firefighter. He has to have toxic masculinity and other associations. I've been enjoying this—too much, probably—but now all I can think about is what that sticker might mean.

If we don't talk about it now, it's going to be on my mind the whole time we're hanging out this morning.

"What's up?" Jake asks, his eyes narrowing slightly.

I take a breath, deciding to confront it head-on before we end up in another location. Depending on how he answers this, I can just turn around and head back inside. "How, like, Red Lives Matter are you?"

Jake looks confused. "I'm a firefighter?"

I point to the sticker. "That has other meanings." I cross my arms, raising my brows.

"Like?" He tilts his head. "What are you getting at?"

Is he playing dumb or does he really not know?

"These flags with a colored stripe were in reaction to the Black Lives Matter movement and feel racist."

"Are you asking me if I'm a racist?"

"Basically."

"I'm not."

I search his eyes, wanting to believe him. There's sincerity there, but I'm not sure if it's enough.

"I give everyone a chance," he adds, breaking the silence. "I don't approach anyone with preconceived notions. I let the scene and environment dictate my assumptions." He pauses, and I keep staring into his eyes, hoping he means every word he's saying. "I don't really forgive, though," he adds. "That's something I should probably work on. Once someone crosses me, they're dead to me."

His words hang in the air, but I'm still unsure. "Well, same here. But ..." I pause, taking a deep breath. "My daughter is of South American descent, so I don't tolerate racism. It's a deal-breaker for me."

"Roger that."

This symbol still rubs me the wrong way.

"Do you really not know about the negative connotation?"

"I mean ... the black flag with the red stripe has been around the entire time I've been a firefighter. So, it wasn't created in response to recent political events. It was already there as a symbol of solidarity and support for firefighters. To me, at the station, with my peers, it's a sign of bravery and sacrifice ... like one of the guy's wives bought all of us these stickers. I see it as a form of pride, but I'll happily get more educated on the topic since it seems like you don't see any of those things when you look at it."

"I didn't know it's been around since before the BLM movement. We'll both have to do more research on this topic then. But it still gives me the ick."

Jake pulls me into a tight hug. I let myself relax against him. That conversation could have gone a lot of ways, but the fact that he said he will do more research gets him points.

Stepping back, I watch him bite his lip. "What? Why are you biting your lip?"

"We're talking about deal-breakers already."

"I guess we're talking about deal-breakers." I laugh softly. "What's one of yours?"

"Well, no drugs. I have to be clean for my job, and even outside of that, I'm not into it."

"I don't do drugs, so no need to worry about that."

"Cool," he says, his smile returning. "And ... I don't want someone who plays games with me. Just be real. No games."

"Got it. No games." I pause, then add, "Anything else?"

He shrugs. "That's about it. What about you?"

I hesitate for a moment, then decide to be honest. "Like I said, racism is a deal-breaker. And I guess ... I don't tolerate dishonesty. I've had enough of that for a lifetime."

"You're going to hate how painfully honest I can be."

Jake leans in to kiss me, cupping my face, and the kiss feels like a promise for everything we've discussed.

I loudly exhale after our kiss ends. "I guess you can play me some country music since we're driving to the lake in your big ass truck."

He chuckles, opening the door for me. I step up and see the to-go coffee cup waiting in the cupholder. *Jake is a nice guy.* Innocent until proven guilty, versus the other way around. He deserves a fair chance.

"Why are you so interested in being with a mess like me?" I ask after taking my first sip.

"I don't think you're a mess."

"Are you lying already?"

"I think you're strong, smart, tenacious, caring ..." He

starts the truck and squeezes my thigh. "Sexy ... you're too gorgeous. I can't get over it."

I smirk, taking another sip of my drink, happy we've cleared the air. I feel lighter, like I can actually enjoy the walk now.

"Are you wearing sunscreen?" I ask, knowing the answer will be no.

"No?"

"Strike one."

"What?"

"You'll have to take sun safety very seriously if we keep dating."

"I'm guessing you burn easily."

"Very. I will forever be as pale as a ghost. Sorry to disappoint."

"Why would that be disappointing?"

"You find girls that glow in the dark sexy?"

He deeply laughs, shaking his head. "I think we've established that I find you very sexy." Sipping my drink, his hand rests on my thigh. "I'll happily rub you down anytime though."

I roll my eyes.

"Corny, I know but I like how big your smile is right now."

I smirk, then stare out the window as we approach, seeing the public beach and Geneva Lake.

"How many miles are you thinking?" he asks, turning off the truck.

"How about let's walk for thirty minutes and then reassess?"

"Works for me."

We hop out of the truck, and he grabs for my hand.

"We're going to hold hands the whole time?" I ask, a bit shocked.

"You're giving me mixed signals here like you want more attention but then when you get it you fight it."

He's right. "I like the attention." I squeeze his hand, and we make our way onto the path. The sun's up for the day and it's already in the seventies. "You're working tonight?"

"Yeah. I have to be on the fireboat by seven."

"Cool."

"If you don't hate me after this walk, let's get brunch somewhere?"

"That sounds great." I smile up at him, looking forward to getting to know him more on this walk. Curious, I ask, "Why did you enlist?"

14

Jake

Why did I enlist in the Marines? "How much time do you have?" I joke, but behind the humor is a question that could be answered in a million different ways. Most of them don't even make sense to me anymore.

"I have at least an hour," she says in a light laugh.

I squeeze her hand as we continue walking along the lakeshore path, the breeze off Geneva Lake cool but comfortable. We're heading toward Williams Bay, though I doubt we'll make it that far. Not that I mind. I could walk for hours with her.

"I enlisted because I wanted to get out of this small town. The challenge seemed cool at first. I was pretty athletic in high school, and I liked the structure sports gave me." I pause, considering how trivial that all seems now. I didn't know what I was signing up for until I was deployed. They don't put the real shit in the brochure, but I don't want to get into all of that. "I didn't have any idea what I'd study in college. I didn't want to rack up a ton of debt."

"Student debt is no joke."

"What did you study?"

"Something extremely employable," she says, deadpan. "Art history."

"Yeah?" I can't help but chuckle. "Did you want to work in a museum or something?"

"I had some big dreams of being a curator or helping artists find their audience. But all it got me was my ex-husband."

"You brought it up." I nudge her gently, wanting to know more. There's a story here, and I want to understand what she's been through. I'm also aware that digging into her last relationship is risky territory, but I need to know who she really is.

"I guess I did." She giggles and pulls her hand away from mine. "I was working at a gallery, and he was this suave older guy that had a really good eye and bought a few things from me."

"How much older are we talking?"

"I met him when I was twenty-three, and he was thirty-eight."

I raise my eyebrows slightly. *That's a decent gap.*

"The security he offered me was more appealing than it should have been. I realize that now."

"Security?"

"I was broke, and here was this guy who was like 'move in with me, let me pay off your student debt, let me make life easier' ..." She trails off.

"So he was a rich older man?"

"The older successful finance guy and the younger creative girl. A stereotype, I know."

"He's South American?" I ask, recalling how she said her daughter is of South American descent.

"Yeah. He was born and raised in Argentina and moved here to get his MBA and then built his career in Chicago."

Hopefully she isn't looking for a guy with money. I do well enough but am not rich by any means, although I'm trying to create more income streams by investing in real estate.

"So, you're in your thirties now?" I've been assuming that.

"Thirty-two. Gabby is four. So if you're trying to do the math in your head ... I got married at twenty-five, had Gabby when I was barely twenty-seven. The divorce started when I was thirty, and here we are."

"In Lake Geneva, Wisconsin of all places." I nudge her before looking out at the lake. There's something grounding about this place, and I wonder if that's part of why she's here—searching for peace.

"I know. I'm still figuring out if small town life is for me, but I do really like it here."

I'm happy she likes it here. "Did you grow up in Chicago?" I ask, because she walks really fast.

"Sort of ... in the suburbs."

"The city has never spoken to me. Not that the Middle East spoke to me or Germany either, but the military brought me to both places." Places I'm perfectly fine leaving in the past.

Her eyes flick to mine. "You were deployed?"

I nod. "Almost the entire time I was in the Marines."

As a group of walkers appears, heading toward us, I instinctively shift behind Claire to give them space. My hands graze the small of her back and lingers on her hips a second too long because I'm staring at her ass. Can't help it. Once they pass, I fall back into step beside her.

"That's kind of crazy," Claire says, glancing over, smiling more than before.

"Definitely," I agree, my voice a little rougher. "Four

years in the military was plenty. After that, I liked the idea of being in service to the community, so yeah ... firefighter."

"Do you like it?"

"Yeah. The best part of my job is when I'm not there, I'm not there."

"Do you have a predictable schedule or is it all over the place?"

"I have seniority, so I have a predictable schedule." It looks like a smile is playing at Claire's lips, but she's holding it back. "Why does that bring a smile to your face?"

"Scheduling is one of life's many challenges."

I squeeze her hand, happy she's thinking about spending more time with me. I'd like to spend more time with her too. Her hand stays in mine, and I let my thumb glide over the soft skin of her knuckles.

"Are you limping?" I ask, noticing her gate change.

"My heel," she mutters, pausing to crouch down. She slips off her shoe and peels her sock at the back. "Shit."

"What's wrong?"

"Blister."

"New shoes?"

"Yeah." She groans.

She can't keep walking on it.

"Piggyback time."

Claire jerks her head up, laughing. "What?"

I crouch down, resting one knee on the dirt path. "Hop on. I'll carry you back to the truck."

"You're not serious."

I glance over my shoulder, grinning. "Why not?"

"It's a long way."

I shrug. "This is basic firefighter training. I'm literally trained to carry people."

She hums like she's considering it, but also clearly resisting.

"You'd rather limp the whole way than let me carry you?"

She shakes her head, a smile tugging at her lips. "Stop trying so hard."

"Why?"

"Because when you stop being cute in three months, it's going to be really annoying."

I smirk. "I'll always be cute."

"Shut up."

"Get on my back already, woman."

She laughs, getting on my back, and for the first time, it feels like we've stopped dancing around something—and stepped right into it.

15

Claire

Climbing onto his back, I am so annoyed with myself. "I hate that I'm always this damsel in distress with you."

He chuckles as he starts walking, the crunch of rocks and twigs under his shoes filling the quiet. Is he seriously going to carry me for over a mile? I smirk, unable to help myself, thinking about his endurance—especially with how solid his back and chest feel beneath me.

"I think you just need to accept the fact that you're not built for solo missions."

"Except for last night," I flirt.

He squeezes my thighs. "So ... what were you thinking about?"

"No. We're not talking about that."

"You're putting the brakes on now?"

I kiss his cheek, looking at the mansions passing by, debating if I'll share a play-by-play of my mission. "You can assume what I was thinking about."

"Why assume?"

I tap his chest. "If you want to know so badly ..." I trail

off, grateful no one is around us. "I was thinking about you shirtless, kissing me everywhere."

"That's sweeter than I'd assumed."

I'm blushing but he can't see it. "So, do you like being in control like that?"

"When it's warranted."

"Warranted?"

"You know what I mean."

"Do I?" I ask coyly, squeezing him tighter.

"Fuck around and find out as they say."

I'm chuckling too much at this conversation. "Aren't you going to ask me if I would even be into that?"

"You're into that," he says, low.

I swat his chest with a little more force this time. "I thought we weren't making assumptions."

"So, you don't want me to take control and turn your brain off from everything else in the world?" I don't know why, but I bite his shoulder. He chuckles. "We can pretend that you're in charge sometimes, but when we're together, *we* know who's in charge."

"Jake ..."

He grumbles.

"So, what's your plan now? Because if it's not to take me back to my place, then I'm going to be upset with you."

"We can't just flirt?"

"Why *just* flirt?"

"Because it's fun."

"Put me down," I say with an edge of sass.

"No."

"Put me down. I don't want you to carry me anymore."

"Claire ..."

"Put me down!"

He sets me down and I wrap my arms around his neck,

kissing him deep. No, he's not going to just flirt with me. No. I'm way too sexually frustrated to just be flirted with. Tugging at his shirt, I could fuck him right on this lake path.

"Claire," he scolds, holding my arms down. Then he smirks and I see the mischief in his eyes. Jake tosses me over his shoulder and spanks my ass hard as he begins walking again.

"Hey!"

"You fucked around and found out."

I'm laughing too much. "I'll get back on your back."

"Nope. You lost those privileges. Now you're a sack of potatoes until we get back."

"Jake!"

He chuckles, and my smile is too big. I like him.

16

Jake

Holding her with one arm over my shoulder, I'm loving this. She's so pissed ... but not actually mad. Claire's not used to yielding. She's just upset that I'm in control.

"If you say something nice to me with no snark, I will give you your piggyback privileges back."

"Pass."

I swat her ass again, and she giggles. We shouldn't sleep together yet, but this has escalated quickly. I'm tempted. "Aren't you going to be embarrassed when other people see me carrying you like this as we re-enter town?"

"Nope. I'll tell everyone you're trying to murder me."

I bend down, putting her back on the ground. Squeezing both of her shoulders with my hands, I look into her big blue eyes. "Claire, can you behave for me?"

"What does behaving look like?"

"Being on my back, not taunting me."

"What's in it for me?"

I lean down, sweetly kissing her. "Brunch, then we can

71

spend the rest of the day doing whatever you want to do." She raises an eyebrow, and I add, "With our clothes on."

"Such a tease."

I shrug. Claire could be end game. There's no way I'm rushing anything. I'm too curious and intrigued and determined to treat her right.

"Cuddling?" she tests.

"I love to cuddle." Although, I know it will escalate if we do. We could touch and kiss, though. Keep it exploratory versus about getting off.

"Watching terrible reality TV?"

"You got it." Honestly, there isn't much I would say no to as long as it means spending more time with her.

She smirks before a big smile grows on her face. "I've been convinced. Let me hop on your back."

17

Claire

Sliding into the booth of the cozy diner for brunch, I've had the best morning with Jake. I haven't been so unburdened and unbothered from life's responsibilities in a long time. Right now, the most difficult thing I'm thinking about is deciding between an omelet and avocado toast. Jake's fingers are distracting me from this simple decision as they trace my hand. Looking up from the menu, he's across from me at the old-school booth, staring at me with the cutest puppy dog expression.

"It was impressive how you carried me so far." He literally carried me to the restaurant. It was mildly embarrassing to be on a grown man's back walking down Main Street, but I liked it.

"Anything for you, Sparky."

"Sparky?" I squint at him, loving the way he's playing with my fingers.

"It's that or firecracker."

I snort. "It's neither of those."

We both laugh softly, and I glance around the busy diner, noting the Fourth of July decorations everywhere, from the plastic star centerpieces to the banners hanging on the walls.

"Oh come on, those are cute nicknames," he says, giving my hand a squeeze.

"Keep working on it."

"Fire starter?"

"I didn't start the fire!" I say, overly dramatic on purpose.

"I know," he says, chuckling under his breath, clearly enjoying this naming game.

"At least you're not calling me Red ... Everyone thinks they are so clever when they call me Red."

Jake leans forward. "Why would they call you Red?" He grabs the end of my ponytail and gives it a playful tug.

"You're into hair pulling, got it," I tease. Not mad to learn this about him. My mind drifts to him shoving my face into a pillow and digging his fingers into my roots. *Focus!*

"So, have you decided?" he asks, leaning back.

"I'll have the western omelet. You?"

"French toast with bacon. Another coffee?"

I nod, and he slides out of the booth, heading up to the counter. I watch him go, smiling to myself, surprised at how easy this all feels. Two hours have flown by.

When he returns, he sets the mug down and extends his other hand toward me. "Here's a Band-Aid for your blister," he says, offering it with a proud grin before leaning down and pressing a kiss to my temple.

Cute. I lean down to put it on my heel as he sits across from me in the booth. When I sit back up, he immediately grabs for my hand again. Staring at him while thinking he's too perfect, I decide to revisit our earlier conversation.

"I want to circle back on something. Let's talk about the stuff you're not supposed to talk about on dates."

"You're having too much fun so you're looking for an out?" He raises a brow, leaning back onto the booth.

"Maybe." I bite my tongue. "But tell me about your political views." I really hope his beliefs are not a deal breaker for me.

"If I had to be lumped into a bucket, then I guess I'm Libertarian."

Interesting. I'm not really familiar with that party. "Why's that?"

"We're adults here, we don't need to be told what to do. I think there should be less attempted parenting in politics."

"That's a good way of putting it ... I try to stay out of politics, but I get so mad about so much that's happening, especially with women's rights."

"I know. In my twenties, I honestly considered running for something. I started getting more involved with local politics and explored what the available positions are. I thought with the military, me being a firefighter, and not unattractive, I could get some traction."

"At least you're self-aware."

"Enough that I have no desire to put my family and friends through that experience. I wouldn't want anyone to get dragged through the mud because I decided to run for something." He pauses, looking thoughtful. "When I was considering that, I decided I value my anonymity more than anything."

Sipping my coffee, I ruminate on all of his words. "Do you want to save the world?"

"I used to. Now I just want to make someone's day better every day. It's an attainable goal."

"You're cute."

"I love when you're nice to me." He squeezes my hand. "So, tell me about your political views?"

"I think women should have full control over their bodies. You could say I'm a single-issue voter on that topic."

"It's good that you vote. Nothing makes me more frustrated than people with lots of opinions who don't vote."

"Same."

My phone buzzes, and stress immediately kicks in. *Is it Gabby's dad?* Is she sick again? Jake's no phones on dates sentiment replays as I stare down at my phone on the table.

"Just look at it," he says with a soft laugh.

"Thanks. Sorry."

NICHOLAS O'MALLEY

Hosting an impromptu barbecue on
Sunday from ten to one. Would love to see
you and Gabby there. I have an exciting
announcement.

Announcement?

"The owner of High Five texted me," I share.

"Nicholas is one of my friends."

"Yeah?" That's another point for Jake. Nicholas is good people. "Everything about this text is suspicious ..."

"Let me see," Jake says, and I cock my head.

"You probably got the text too."

"No phones on dates." He winks, then extends his hand, and I give him my phone.

"I have an idea," he says coyly, looking down at the screen.

What could Nicholas be announcing? My gut is telling me it has to do with Emily.

"Me too ... but would he really get engaged after seven months of being official?"

"When you know, you know," Jake says, far too casually.

"Do you really believe that?"

"Yes."

Jake's sincerity and eye contact are unreal. "So ... since you want to spend so much time with me, what do you think about going to that barbecue on Sunday?"

"As a date?" he playfully asks.

"Yes."

"I'd love that."

"Is it okay if I text Nicholas back?"

"Asking for permission." Jake bites his lip. "Such a good girl." I shake my head, blushing while texting.

CLAIRE MOORE

> See you then. Your place? Gabby is with her dad, but I'll be arriving with your friend Jake.

NICHOLAS O'MALLEY

> Not at my place. Long story, but my sister's friend owns a house on the lake and offered it to us for the party. I'll text you the address. And Jake Schmidt?

"Is your last name Schmidt?" I ask, looking up from my phone, feeling embarrassed I didn't ask yet.

"Yeah."

CLAIRE MOORE

> Yes. That Jake.

NICHOLAS O'MALLEY

> Good guy. Tell him Chad and Chris will be there too.

I hit the thumbs up reaction. "Nicholas wants me to tell you that Chad and Chris will be there."

"Nice!" Jake squeezes my hand. "I'm sure you're still getting used to small town life, where everyone knows everyone's business."

"Still getting used to it, yes. Same Chad whose truck got pranked?"

"Yeah."

"Oh ... small towns."

Leaving the diner, he asks, "Could you share an ice cream?"

"Aren't you full?"

"That's why I'm offering to share." The smile on his face. I can't get over how much of a Golden Retriever he can be sometimes. I've never dated a guy like this. "I feel like we have to do it," he says. "It's the fourth."

"We can share an ice cream as long as it's not Superman or mint flavored."

"Should we get vanilla?" He winks.

"I'm open." I smirk, liking the thought of what a relationship with Jake could look like.

Jake grabs my chin, leaning down for a firm kiss. "Isn't today the best day?"

"It's really nice. You're doing a good job of keeping my brain off."

He grumbles before whispering, "I know, look how nice you're being to me."

I swat his chest, and he chuckles, leading us to the ice cream shop on the corner of Main Street.

"Sea salt caramel?" he asks, and honestly, that is the perfect choice.

"My favorite."

We wait in the line, and he stands behind me hugging

me tight. This is a fantasy. Almost seventy-two hours of not being a mom. Not needing to work.

What will this be like when reality kicks back in?

Jake kisses the top of my head. "Stop stressing."

"How do you know I'm stressed?" I whisper, looking up at him.

"You're not really a quiet person unless you're deep in thought."

He's got me there. Jake orders for us and pays. "Thank you."

"Anytime," he says, grabbing my hand, leading us to the other side of the shop to wait for the ice cream. "What trashy reality TV show is in our future?"

"I haven't watched something that isn't animated in months, so whatever new dating show is on Netflix."

"Why a dating show?"

"They're always so bad, and we can make bets about who is and isn't going to work out."

He chuckles, taking the ice cream from the worker. Extending it to me, I lick a little and then he bites into it, staring at me. I flinch, watching that.

"How can you bite into ice cream?" I ask, still feeling tingles in my body because my teeth are too sensitive to ever bite into ice cream.

He bites it again, holding eye contact with me. Well, that's hot. Jake hands me the cone, and we walk outside. Strolling along the sidewalk, stealing the cone from each other as we walk, I love this. Today has been fun. I can't remember the last time I had this much fun.

18

Jake

On Claire's couch, she's leaning her head on my shoulder watching some dating show where everyone has a British accent. Every time she laughs, I smile. Scanning her living room, I spot the brown teddy bear I bought for Gabby sitting at a play table and chair set across from a doll. I'm happy she's having fun with it. There are tons of toys in this room. The toy organizer is over-flowing with toys all around it. This house feels like it's well set up for a kid, but it's lacking personal touches. No decor, no flowers on the kitchen counter. I don't see Claire anywhere. I can't imagine how hard it is doing everything on her own.

"Can I give you a shoulder massage?" I softly ask. She nods, and I kiss the top of her head. "Let me get behind you."

We maneuver around on the couch until she's comfortably sitting between my legs, still watching the TV. As I start gently rubbing her shoulders, I notice how tense she is —muscles knotted, shoulders tight. She leans back as I press deeper, melting into my touch.

"We're just going to cuddle and watch trashy TV?" she skeptically asks.

"We'll do whatever keeps you relaxed and smiling."

"Well ..." A smirk grows on her face before she giggles.

"So needy," I whisper, continuing to massage her. "I don't have anything I have to do tomorrow, you know..." I add, letting the thought hang in the air.

"You want to see me tomorrow?"

"Yes."

"That's three days in a row, Jake," she says, sounding both amused and a little apprehensive.

I laugh. "Well, it could be four. We're going to Nicholas's barbecue on Sunday." She looks over her shoulder, staring at me skeptically, but then a smile consumes her face. "How about this? What's your dream 'me day' look like?"

"Um, wake up, get a fancy coffee like something I can't make at home, read my book on the couch until I want to take a bath."

"Tomorrow. You're doing that and then, if you'd like, I'll come over and make you dinner." I squeeze her shoulders slightly and feel them relax under my hands, like the idea is already relaxing her.

"Sounds good." Claire leans into me, tilting her head back. "Later ... when do you need to leave for work?"

"I should leave here at five. There's a few things I need to accomplish before work."

"So ..." she hesitates, tilting her head back, searching my face, "we're just watching TV until then?"

"Tell me what you'd rather do." My voice is a bit lower than I intended, but I'm curious. I want her to say what she's thinking.

"You know what I want to do."

"I'd rather not assume."

She rolls her eyes playfully and turns around, crawling into my lap until she's straddling me. Her eyes narrow. "Is this your kink?"

"Is what my kink?" I ask, my hands squeezing her hips.

"Having me tell you what I want."

"Maybe," I whisper, taking out her ponytail and playing with her hair, brushing it behind her shoulders. "You should just tell me, so I'll do it."

"But then where's the mystery?" Her eyes flicker with that same playful spark, and her lips are teasingly close to mine.

"Do you want mystery, or do you want to know exactly what's going to happen?"

Claire bites her lip before kissing me. Leaning back, she asks, "How ... Dom are you?"

"It depends. Everyone's different, you know?" Claire's lips tease my neck, and I pull her closer to me. "I like things to be playful, more than just control and submission."

She squints at me, and I'm curious. I don't get strong Sub vibes from her. Not that it really matters. But she's definitely a brat.

"I won't wear a collar," she says, watching me carefully, like she's setting a boundary.

"Oh, I'm not that hardcore." I laugh, wrapping my hands around her wrist and placing them on my shoulders. "I'm interested in connection more than anything."

She raises an eyebrow. "What else do you get up to?"

"Plenty," I whisper and press my forehead to hers, and she laughs softly, bringing me into a kiss.

When she breaks our kiss, she sighs loudly. "Let's be real. When this bubble of me not working and not having to be a mom pops ... I don't know what this will look like."

I pull her in for a big hug. She wants this. She wants something more than a hookup. "It'll look however you want it to," I say softly into her hair, squeezing her.

She shakes her head slightly. "You might only get to see me one night a week at most."

"Better than not seeing you at all."

She narrows her eyes at me. "You're all in on this?"

"I'm all in," I say, shrugging because I don't know how to be any other way. I've never been able to date multiple people at once. "That's how I roll."

She looks thoughtful for a moment, then leans back, studying my face. "So, when was your last relationship?"

"There was a girl I dated for a couple of months, but ... she wasn't the one. So I broke it off." Thinking back to it, I tried a lot of new things with her, but it affirmed that I want a more traditional relationship with a partner.

"You're looking for 'the one'?"

"Aren't we all?" As I say it, I hope Claire is. I hope she could be ready for something serious because everything about our time together says this could work. But I'll take whatever I can get from her in the meantime.

"I don't know..." She sighs, glancing away. "I don't know if 'the one' is a thing."

I study her, trying to read the expression she's not sharing with me. "Are you anti-marriage now that you've been there and done that?"

"Not anti, just ... cautious." She pauses, looking down. "Marriage is a business partnership. I used to see it like a fairytale, but now... I'd need to know everything if I ever went down that road again. Like, bank statements, credit scores—I won't enter anything blind."

I chuckle, appreciating the realness. "I have almost a perfect credit score. A mortgage well within my means. But cars ... okay, cars are where I light a lot of money on fire, but it's never more than I can afford."

We fall quiet again, her still straddling me, and I know we've barely scratched the surface here. Rubbing my hands up and down her arms, I'm happy she's letting me in, keeping her guard lowered. I know this might bring back the defenses, but we're talking about all of this.

"Can I ask what your situation is with your ex ... like financially?"

She huffs, closing her eyes for a moment before saying, "Since I have primary custody, he pays me child support and I also have alimony. He thinks it's more than enough for me to live some fabulous life, but it barely covers the basic expenses like rent, food, and everything. But ... it is enough that I don't have to work forty hours, which is really amazing for me and Gabby."

"It's good to hear that he isn't a deadbeat."

"He isn't a deadbeat, but he *is* an asshole. I'm pretty sure he moved a lot of money around to try to act like he has less than he does. I mean ... our life together was a lot more extravagant. It's so frustrating that he wouldn't want to give us ... give Gabby more. Like the guy goes out for two-hundred-dollar dinners multiple times a week but when I ask for a couple hundred dollars for dance lessons, it's a whole production."

I bear hug her, squeezing her tight.

"I'm tired of asking," she says, resting her head on my shoulder. "So I don't ask unless I really need it. It's not worth the stress and all the other emotions that come up."

"Gabby's lucky to have a mom like you." I cup her face in my hand and kiss her deep. "The effort you put in is all around, and I know she is your top priority."

"Thanks ... it's really hard. But I want her to have a nice

childhood." Claire looks down. "Dating me means that you get all the baggage."

"I understand you're a multidimensional person."

"My ex is really triggering, so you're going to get annoyed with me about that."

I chuckle. "What else will I get annoyed by?"

"The lack of time I have for you."

I flip her over so her back is on the couch. "I like when you're real with me." I run my tongue along her neck, and she squirms. Hovering above her, I instruct, "Keep talking."

19

Claire

"You're going to hate how I organize. I always have piles." I giggle, turned on by the way Jake's touching and kissing me. "It's my way of organizing before I actually do it."

"Clutter is annoying." He smirks, then crashes his lips into mine. He is a great kisser. "But ... worth it," he says, pulling back.

Tugging at his shirt, it needs to come off.

"I also really like foreplay," he says, pinning my arms down, not letting me take his shirt off. "You're going to have to accept that I move slow."

I huff, although I am not complaining. I'm sweating. I love the way he takes control. Releasing my wrists, his hands explore my body as he's kissing all over my neck. His lips move up my jaw and then deeply kiss me. It's teasing, but it's taking my breath away.

Jake leans back, looking into my eyes, smiling down at me. "You're so beautiful. I love your freckles," he says, swiping his thumb across my cheek. "You already know I love your hair, but it's amazing."

"You will probably be annoyed with how long it takes to tame," I say, staring into his blue eyes, loving the sight of him hovering above me.

He cocks his head. "Is it naturally curlier than this?" he asks, grabbing at the ends of my hair, and all I can think about is how long it's been since I got a haircut.

"It wants to be Shirley-Temple-level curly but that is too much."

"Mmm ... I'll need to see it."

"We could shower ..." I test. "Then you would see it."

"I want to be naked with you, but isn't this fun?" He lifts my shirt, trailing his tongue up my stomach.

"Fun for who?" I sass, but this is great. Jake kissing and licking my hips and stomach is a lot of fun.

"Why does sex have to have a goal?" he asks, flicking his eyes up to meet mine.

A goal? "What do you mean?" I ask softly.

"Don't be so focused on the finish line." He places three baby kisses up my hip, before adding, "There's so much more to intimacy."

I think I get what he's saying, but I also might be reading it wrong. "What are you saying?"

"Have you ever heard of Tantra or Tantric sex?" he asks, leaning back and holding my gaze.

"No," I say, dragging out the word playfully because whatever that is, it sounds interesting.

"Well ... you should read about it, and basically it's all about prolonged experiences that are not about the end game of an orgasm, rather more about bonding and intimacy."

"How did Jake the firefighter discover he likes this?" I ask flirtily.

"I'm open minded and attract open minded people." He

squeezes me. "I understand you can't have hours every time to be intimate, but when there's time, like there is now, I think it's the best."

"So what do you want to do with me?" I ask, grinning.

"I want to kiss you, touch you, tickle you ... caress every inch of you. I want to learn your body."

"Okay ..." I whisper hesitantly but need to shelve my insecurities about him exploring me with this level of detail because I want him to touch me.

"We could also do some breathing stuff, but I think that might be best for another time."

"Why's that?"

"Because I see your guard's going back up a little ... so foreplay ... I want to do that for a while."

"I am, what, laying here on the couch while you explore?"

"We can go to the bed, but know that my dick will not be involved at all."

"I would rather be in my bed."

"Then, let's go to your bed."

20

Jake

"Do you want to, like, really try this?" I ask as she sits at the foot of the bed. I quickly scan the room. The comforter is quilted and plush. The walls are white. She hasn't decorated this room either. I wonder what her plans are, when her lease expires. I hope she wants to stay in Wisconsin because my life is here.

"As long as it involves your hands and lips, yes," she says, her blue eyes looking up at me with hunger.

I stare down at her, and she leans back onto her forearms a little more. "Eye contact is important. So don't close your eyes. I know it's instinct, but I want you to keep looking at me."

"The *whole* time?" she breathes, surprised.

I smile. "Eye contact is great for bonding."

"Okay," she says with a questioning edge.

"Would you be more comfortable under the covers or lying on top of them?"

"Under the covers."

"Do you feel self-conscious? Because there is nothing to be self-conscious about." I pull up her shirt and drop it on

89

the floor. Taking her in, I smile and lean down to kiss her lips. "You are so fucking sexy."

"I'm trying not to be self-conscious," she says between kisses. "But I also get cold easily."

"Then get under the covers, Sparky."

"You're not calling me that."

"But I like it," I tease as I take off my shirt and slide in on the other side of the bed. Her eyes go wide before she asks, "When were you going to tell me you have tattoos?" Claire traces my chest piece with her fingers while lying on her side.

"I forget about them, honestly."

Slowly, she examines the black and white compass that bleeds into a map of the world on my shoulder.

"Semper Fi," she says, her finger gliding over the black ink above the compass.

"My first tattoo." I shrug. "Eighteen and in the marines. Felt like the right idea."

"You don't like it now?" She props her head up, resting it in her hand as she lays on her side.

"I like that it translates to: Always Faithful." I lean in to kiss her. "Because I am."

She smirks, breaking my gaze. I grab her chin, and she looks back into my eyes. "Your eyes are amazing." She softly closes them. "They are. So, do you still want to try something new?" She nods. "Think about being in high school when you were too nervous to do more than just kiss and touch. It's like that, but without the awkwardness."

"Well, I'm still a little insecure. Especially compared to you."

"Why?" I glide my hand down her leg, wanting her to feel like the sexiest person alive because she is.

"I'm soft. You're ... well, an action figure."

"Soft where?" I squeeze the inside of her thigh, and she lets out a small sound. "I like that you're soft." I brush my fingers over her skin again, watching her reaction. "You like when I touch your thigh here?" I ask, caressing her inner thigh.

"Yes," she breathes out and I love that sound. She's relaxing.

"How's the eye contact?" I ask, grinning as I kiss the strap of her bra.

"I'm getting used to it."

"Good. Keep at it." I trail my fingers up her stomach, watching her squirm slightly when I reach her ribs. "Learning your body is fun. Every reaction makes me want to learn more."

I slide one strap of her bra down, kissing the skin it leaves behind. "You're beautiful."

She smiles softly, and I reach behind her, unclasping her bra. She moves to cover herself, but I gently stop her hand. "Let me." I ease it off, my gaze lingering on her. My pulse picks up. I kiss across her chest, then flick my tongue over her nipple, watching the way her breath catches. There's something intoxicating about the look in her eyes— like she's teetering between trust and desire. "I like that you're not used to taking it slow."

I smile against her skin, kissing my way down her stomach. *Claire could be the one.* The thought keeps popping into my head. She is the kind of partner I want: strong, passionate, loving, easy to be with ... and too fucking gorgeous. I reach her hip bone, and she tilts her head back, closing her eyes.

"Look at me," I whisper.

Her lashes flutter open as I trail my tongue up her stomach, claiming her lips in a deep kiss.

"Roll over."

"Why?"

"I need to continue exploring."

"What about you?"

"This isn't about me." I press a kiss to the center of her back, smiling when she wiggles beneath me.

"It tickles," she laughs, shifting.

"Tickles, huh?" I run my fingers lightly down her spine, stopping at the curve of her waist. She squirms again. I can't hold back a smile.

I pull the covers down more, admiring her in her bike shorts. "You have a great ass." I playfully swat her, then place soft kisses along the fabric until I reach her bare thigh. Every movement, every little reaction, makes me want to know her even more—every part of her, not just this. I bring the covers back up so she doesn't get cold.

"Look at me," I say softly. She turns to her side, locking eyes with me. "I really like this. Just touching and playing around."

"It's nice," she says with a soft smile. Claire slips her hand under my waistband. Her eyes narrow slightly. "You're not hard."

I chuckle, grabbing her wrist and pinning it back as I roll on top of her. "Because that's not what we're doing."

"But ... you're touching me."

"Self-restraint. I have a lot of it."

She pouts, and I kiss her bottom lip, then cup her between her legs, feeling her warmth through the fabric. "Is this all you want from me?"

"No," she breathes, and I run my hand up her body.

"I want to wait," I say, rubbing my thumb along her jaw. I want our connection to be more than sex and am afraid if we go there now, it will cloud things between us. "I want to keep kissing and touching, but not there. Not yet."

"Okay."

I lean in, my lips brushing against her ear. "Once I taste you, there's no going back."

Her breath hitches, and I press another kiss to her lips as we hold unrelenting eye contact. I feel our connection growing, like we're silently exchanging a knowing understanding of how special this bond is. It's beyond physical—something deeper, something rare. The energy between us pulses, and I feel completely in sync with her, and nothing else exists in this moment.

21

Claire

"I want to try this breathing thing you've talked about," I say softly, melting into him.

Jake smiles, pushing the covers back as he sits up. "Breathing together is really intimate. You're going to feel things. It's intense."

"I'm ready."

"Wrap your legs around my waist."

I do, and he takes my hand, placing it over his heart before resting his own hand on top of mine. I stare at his chest and admire how the tattoos cover his pec and shoulder and go into a quarter sleeve. His skin is warm, his heartbeat steady beneath my palm. The connection is instant. Strong. Already, the air between us shifts—heavier, more charged.

"Eye contact," he reminds me, his voice softer now. My gaze shifts between his eyes. "Breathe with me. Inhale ..."

I follow his lead, taking a deep, slow breath. My chest lifts in time with his.

"Exhale."

We let go together, and something inside me unwinds. The second inhale comes easier, deeper. His breath becomes mine, and mine his. We are moving together, no longer needing words—rising, falling, sharing. I notice the different shades of blue in his eyes and how he has a darker circle around his iris. My body feels lighter, like I'm floating against him. A warmth spreads through my core, a tingle settling low in my belly. My skin buzzes where we touch, but it's more than physical—it's like we're exchanging something unseen, a knowing energy passing between us.

Jake's fingers graze my back, bringing me closer to him with each breath. His eyes stay locked on mine. "It's nice to be intimate in a way that doesn't involve an orgasm," he says, pressing a tender kiss to my forehead.

I smile, completely in tune with him now. The world outside of this moment fades, leaving just *us*—our breath, our bodies, the heat between us.

"One more," he whispers.

Our final inhale is deep, full. As we exhale, he slides his hands up, cupping my face before capturing my lips in a deep, intentional kiss.

He wraps his arms around me as he falls back onto the bed, pulling me on top of him. "You're a natural," he says with a satisfied smile. "Our connection is rare," he breathes, holding me tight against his chest.

"I liked that a lot," I say softly. "It's feels like I've known you for more than a couple of days," I say, snuggling into his chest, trailing my fingers up his bicep.

I can't remember the last time I felt this relaxed.

"Your mission tonight is to finish the show we were watching and tell me who ends up together," Jake says, breaking our makeout session at the front door.

"Okay." I smile, feeling light, relaxed—peaceful after hours of cuddling and kissing.

"Bye." He lingers in the doorway, dipping back in for another sweet kiss. "Enjoy your 'me day' tomorrow," he says, his fingers squeezing me at my waist.

"I will."

"You can tell me how the show ends while I'm cooking you dinner tomorrow."

I nod, and the warmth in his eyes is making me melt. "I want you to bring me a copy of the department calendar too," I add, because I really want to see what Jake's photo looks like.

"Anything for you." He squeezes my hand. "I don't want to leave," he whispers, pulling me in again, tighter. "I miss you already."

I smile against his chest. "Red, you have some work to do."

"Red?"

I smirk. "If you're going to call me Sparky, then I'm calling you Red."

"Because I'm a firefighter?"

"Because that's what I'm going to call you," I say playfully.

He chuckles, then cups my face, his thumbs brushing softly over my cheekbones. "Bye." Another lingering kiss, then he steps back.

I watch as he opens the door and leaves, stifling the urge to call him for another kiss. Instead, I close the door, leaning against it for a second to relish in the day. My body still tingles from his touch. My face hurts from smiling.

I grab a bag of popcorn and toss it in the microwave, but my thoughts drift.

I'm falling for Red. Jake the firefighter. Captain America. The guy who kisses me like I've never been kissed. Who wants to explore my body for hours without needing to take more. Who holds me like he doesn't want to let go.

The microwave beeps, shaking me from my thoughts. Popcorn in hand, I snuggle into the couch, queuing up the dating show, but my mind isn't on it.

Who even cares who ends up together on this stupid show? I'm too focused on if I'm ready to end up with Jake Schmidt.

22

Jake

"What's that skip in your step about?" my fire chief, Bill, asks from the new aluminum fireboat—courtesy of donations and the successful calendar fundraiser.

"I met a girl!" I yell, walking down the creaky wood pier, smiling at the old man as I approach in my department T-shirt, khakis, and steel-toed boots.

"Oh yeah?" he asks skeptically as I hop into the boat, nodding as I do.

"Sup, March?" I ask, fist bumping our newest and youngest firefighter, Olivia, who is also on firework duty.

She gives me a nod as Bill taps his fingers on his lips, looking deep in thought. "This girl is special?" he asks after a few moments.

"Very."

"Tell her she can watch the fireworks from the boat as long as she can get here in the next fifteen minutes."

My heart pounds with excitement. "Yeah?"

"Get calling."

I pull out my phone and immediately dial Claire. *Please pick up.*

"You miss me already?" she teases, answering.

"Yes, and if you are not sick of me yet ... want to watch the fireworks from the lake?" I ask, speaking fast because we are on a time crunch.

"I thought you were working," she says, her pitch rising.

"I am, but my chief offered ... you have to be here in less than fifteen minutes."

"Um."

There's a beat of silence. "I know," I exhale, thinking she's going to reject this idea. "You can say no."

"That sounds really fun." I hear the excitement in her voice, and it makes me grin from ear to ear.

"Bring a blanket and snacks, and know that if you have to pee, you'll have to put your butt in the water."

"Got it. Will pee now." She giggles. "I'll be right over."

She hangs up, and I look at Bill, giving him a fist bump. "Thank you for being my wingman here."

"This job is for insurance ... I'm not concerned, so you two sit on the front of the boat, and Olivia and I will stay out of your way back here." He pauses. "Olivia, do you have anyone special you want to bring out?"

"Special?" She laughs. "No."

"Are you playing the field?" he asks in a laugh.

"I'm allowing men to buy me food since I'm so fucking underpaid."

We both laugh. "Are you saying if I gave you a promotion, you wouldn't be dating?"

"I would take the promotion over this never-ending line of losers I'm meeting online."

Bill's head turns, looking at me now. "Jake, do you know anyone?"

I cock a brow. "Why are you playing matchmaker?"

"I was at my grandson's baptism this morning, and I

want everyone to settle down and start a family. It's the best part of life."

Olivia and I glance at each other, finding this soft side of Bill odd.

"How old is too old for you, Olivia?" I ask, thinking she's maybe twenty-four.

"I'm not an ageist unless he's, like, fetishizing my youth."

Bill and I chuckle. "Well ... I'll keep that in mind, but all of my friends are either married or in serious relationships."

"Now back to business," Bill says, clapping his hands for emphasis. "Olivia, run through the checklist to make sure we have everything onboard. Jake, test out each of the fire hoses and lights to confirm they are working properly."

I waste no time getting to work.

"Claire," I yell, seeing her on the pier. She waves, a blanket draped over one arm and a large tote slung over the other shoulder. Red hair, white shorts, and a blue sweatshirt. *Patriotic*, I think with a smirk.

I extend a hand to help her into the boat. We exchange a smile, and once she's on board, I kiss the top of her head. "This is Bill and Olivia."

They nod, Bill shooting me an approving glance. I lead her to the front of the boat, and we sit on the bow.

With my arm around her shoulder, I whisper, "I'm so happy you were able to make it." I'm completely relaxed, wrapped in this picturesque moment—us cuddled on the bow as the sun dips low on the horizon. Claire nuzzles into me, and the boat's engines come to life.

Bill and Olivia untie us from the pier, and Bill steers us toward the middle of the lake where the barge will launch the fireworks. It's one of the busiest days of the year out here. Boats glide past, each with its own soundtrack blaring. The water is choppy, sending the occasional spray of mist our way.

Claire smirks up at me.

"What?" I whisper.

"Earlier was fun."

"Very." I kiss the top of her head as the boat rocks, hitting another wave. "I could kiss you forever."

She rests her head on my shoulder, and I squeeze her closer. A boat zooms past us, too close, and I groan. "Little shits."

Olivia is already on the megaphone. "One hundred feet, frat stars!"

The other boat goes in neutral, the guy behind the wheel asking, "What's that, princess?"

I huff, unwrapping my arm from Claire and stand. My eyes inventory the group. Each guy is holding a beer. "What did she tell you?" I call out.

The boat is silent until the guy says, "One hundred feet."

"Right. Stay one hundred feet from other moving boats."

Then I look back at Olivia and nod at Bill. He grabs the radio and calls the police boat, sharing this boat's registration number.

"Drunks are the worst," I softly say, sitting back down with Claire.

"What's it like getting people to shape up just by putting your attention on them?"

"You tell me." I wink, wrapping my arm around her shoulders and pulling her in tight.

"Any minute now," I say, glancing at my phone for a brief moment—8:30 p.m.

With the sun setting and Claire in my arms, this is perfect. Today has been the perfect day with the perfect woman. The lake is still, the waves have calmed, and every boat sits in silence, engines off, waiting for the show.

As the first firework explodes above us, I glance at Claire. The white light flickers across her face, her lips slightly parted as she watches the sky in awe. She looks completely at peace, even with the loud echo from the blast reverberating across the lake. I get lost in her beauty and aura until my mind says, *I've fallen.*

I've more than fallen.

The past couple of days have been a fever dream, but the kind I never want to wake up from. I want more of this —more nights, more memories, more of her.

"I can come by every evening to give you a kiss goodnight," I whisper, the words slipping out before I can stop them.

Claire tilts her head, looking at me like she didn't hear me right. "What?"

"You said you don't have a lot of time. But I can see you every night. Even if it's just for a few minutes. I don't care if we can only go out once a week—I still want to see you. I want this."

She blinks, stress emerging on her face as another loud boom and crackle fill the silence.

I press on, my heart pounding. "I want to give this a go."

She's quiet, and we hold unwavering eye contact as the red and blue fireworks reflect in her eyes.

"You're asking me to be your girlfriend?" she finally asks, a mixture of surprise and something else—something unreadable—crossing her face.

I grab her hand. "If you want to be in a relationship, I'd love for you to be my girlfriend."

Claire lets out a small laugh, shaking her head. "Jake ... we just met."

"I know," I say with a small smile. "I can be a softie. But I know what I want."

She bites her lip, clearly thinking. Then she leans in, pressing a soft kiss to my cheek. "Let's see how the barbecue goes on Sunday."

23

Claire

Am *I really about to be Jake's girlfriend?*
The thought loops in my mind as the finale of the fireworks explodes across the sky. The red, white, and blue colors of the fireworks reflect in the lake, but I can barely focus. Jake is great—more than great. But this is fast. Too fast. I've done fast before, and it's always led to heartbreak. I need to slow down.

I lean closer into him. *God, he feels good.* And I know that's part of the problem. It's easy to get lost in him. His big arms and strong chest. The way his arm is around me, holding me like I'm something precious, in the way his kisses leave me breathless. But he hasn't seen my real life yet. He hasn't seen me juggling work shifts, daycare pickups, and exhaustion. Does he really know what he's asking?

"We're not rushing," I whisper, looking up at him, smoke from the fireworks illuminated by the stars.

He leans down, kissing my forehead.

As the boat joins a slow procession heading back toward the pier, my mind races. Am I ready for a boyfriend? *Do* I want a boyfriend? Jake is incredible. But ... my life.

When we dock, I step off the boat and wave to the others before Jake and I walk together toward my car. I am flirting with a lot of things right now. It will be good to have a "me day" tomorrow to be with all of my thoughts.

The sound of the water lapping against the shore fades behind us, replaced by the dull hum of crickets and distant laughter from the crowd still lingering by the pier. We walk in silence for a few moments until I find the courage to say it. "I really like you, Jake."

"I know."

I swat his arm, but I'm already smiling. "I don't want to rush into a relationship," I admit. "That's my move. That's what I typically do, and I can't do that anymore."

Jake nods. "I get it. You know where I stand. When you're ready, I'm ready."

Why does that make me want him more?

I hesitate, biting my lip, wanting to invite him back to my place—to stretch out this night, to keep feeling his hands on me, his lips tracing my skin. "Come back to my place?"

"Not tonight."

I arch a brow. "Are you withholding sex until I'm your girlfriend?"

Jake doesn't answer with words. Instead, he steps closer, crowding me against the car. His hand slides along my jaw, tilting my face up toward him. And then he kisses me—deep, slow, consuming. His force presses me back against the door. I'm lost in this moment. Completely lost in the way his tongue traces against mine, in the way his body feels solid and unmovable against me.

He pulls back just enough to murmur against my lips, "We're not rushing. I'm respecting your wishes."

I groan, hating and loving his restraint all at once.

Jake smirks, brushing one last kiss against my forehead. "Goodnight, Sparky. Enjoy your 'me day' tomorrow."

I watch as he walks away, my heart pounding in my chest. I should feel relieved that he's giving me space. But all I feel is the ache of wanting more.

24

Jake

Claire's nervous to make this official, and I can't believe I'm thinking she could be the one. I've never felt this way before. I know she's on vacation from her day-to-day life, but I see us. I see our life together. And I *want* it.

As I drive home, my thoughts race, replaying all of our time together. I tap my mom's contact. It's late, but I need to cancel family dinner.

She picks up after a few rings, her voice groggy through the car's Bluetooth. "Jake?"

"Sorry for calling so late. I'm not going to be able to make it for dinner tomorrow."

"Everything alright?" She's more alert now.

"Yeah. Everything's great, actually. I'll be cooking dinner for someone special."

"Oh?" Her voice lifts, the sleepiness fading.

"Her name is Claire. I think she could be *the one*."

Silence stretches for a moment. Then another.

"The one?" she echoes. "Jake, I've never heard you say that before."

I nervously adjust my grip on the wheel. "I know." No

one has ever made me feel this way. I started telling myself that maybe I was looking for a feeling that wasn't real, that was only told in stories, but then I met Claire.

Mom exhales. Then her tone softens. "So, what are you cooking for this special girl?"

"Haven't decided yet."

"Something easy for conversation. Maybe garlic herb chicken with vegetables in a slow cooker—something you can set and forget."

I smile. "That's a great idea. I'll make that." I can already picture Claire sitting at her table, the smell of thyme and garlic filling her home. It feels right. "Love you, Mom. I'll let you get back to sleep."

"Oh no." She laughs. "You can't tell me you think you've found the one and leave it at that. Tell me about her."

I chuckle, rubbing the back of my neck. "Her name's Claire. I met her after she called 911—there was a small fire at High Five."

"Oh. How's Nicholas?"

"He's good. The women's bathroom was out of commission for a couple of days, but it's back in action now."

"That's good to hear." She pauses. "And Claire?"

"She's the most beautiful woman I've ever seen. Red hair, freckles—gorgeous. But it's more than that. The way she handled herself during the fire ... I was instantly drawn to her. We've been out a couple times now since her daughter's with her dad for the weekend. She's funny, caring, and passionate. I don't know—I just ... it's different in a good way."

Mom is quiet for a moment, then gently asks, "How old is her daughter?"

"Four."

"That's a big responsibility ..."

"I know."

"Divorce ..." Another pause, then a long exhale. "Just be careful, okay?"

I sigh. "I know. Claire is too. She's cautious—guarded, even. I'm taking things slow."

"Divorces bring a lot into a relationship." Mom hesitates. "Make sure you're not the only one all-in."

I swallow, rolling my shoulders back. I feel Claire pulling away at times. She's not jumping in the way I am. But when she looks at me, when she leans into my touch, when she softens in my arms ... she wants this. Even if she's scared.

"She's worth the wait." She is. Even if she doesn't want to be my girlfriend right now. I will wait until she is ready.

"Good. Bring her to family dinner soon."

I love that idea and can't wait for Claire and my relationship to be there. And if I'm not getting too ahead of myself, I can't wait for all three of us to share this tradition.

25

Claire

Saturday, July 5th

A me day. A day for me to do whatever I want, whenever I want. I roll over and tap my phone: 7:45 a.m. My days of sleeping in are long gone. My internal clock since having Gabby is too rewired. I rub my eyes, then type out a quick text to Jake.

CLAIRE MOORE

> Morning! What time are you coming over to play chef?

I shouldn't feel awkward that I didn't agree to be his girlfriend last night, but I do.

JAKE SCHMIDT

> Whenever you want. Maybe 4:30?

I tap the thumbs-up reaction and sink into the abyss of TikTok, mindlessly scrolling for too long. Throwing off the covers, I slide out of bed. Hair in a messy bun, oversized athleisure on, I start thinking about where to get coffee until my phone buzzes.

> **JAKE SCHMIDT**
> Coffee delivery. Look outside.

What?

I step to my front door, and there it is, a to-go coffee waiting on the front stoop. I look around. No Jake. I pick it up and sip. Vanilla latte, like yesterday. But it tastes even better today.

The surprise. The foreseeing of my needs. He's spoiling me. Campaigning to be my boyfriend. He's embodying "if he wanted to he would." Smiling, I take another sip.

> **CLAIRE MOORE**
> You're sweet.

> **JAKE SCHMIDT**
> Time for you to sit on the couch and read.

I smirk and curl up on the couch, tucking a blanket around me. I try to focus on my book, but my mind keeps drifting to Jake.

The way he looks at me. The way he listens. The way he makes me feel like I am something worth waiting for.

I sip my coffee, letting my thoughts drift to a mental list:

- **Pro:** There's no one else. I'm only interested in him.
- **Pro:** He's thoughtful, dependable, and easy to be around.
- **Con:** My life is complicated. Being with me isn't just being with me. It means understanding my schedule, my responsibilities, my past.

- **Con:** Can I handle adding someone else's needs into my daily life?

The truth is, I'm not just afraid of things moving fast. I'm afraid of losing myself again. It's more than my ex. It's my lack of parents too. I've experienced so much loss and don't know if I can handle any more.

I toss the blanket aside. I'm too restless to sit still. If I can't quiet my mind, I can at least tire out my body. I cast a bodyweight workout onto the TV and push through squats, lunges, and burpees. It's been a while since I've done this, but I missed it.

Maybe I should start working out a couple of times a week again. I know it's healthy and what I should be doing, but I also don't want to be this soft anymore, even if Jake likes it.

I laugh to myself as I walk to the bathroom, sweaty and satisfied. Jake is the first guy who hasn't made little comments about how I could look better. My ex was always saying something—*"Are you sure you want to eat that?"* Meanwhile, Jake keeps feeding me. I can't wait to see what he's making for dinner.

I turn the handle on the tub and gather candles. It's been forever since I've had a long bath. I chuckle as I light a few. *I probably shouldn't burn the place down.* But I keep lighting them anyway.

Jake in his fire suit ... now that's some roleplay we'll to have to explore.

I step into the steaming water, the scent of lavender wrapping around me from the bath bomb. My muscles relax, but my mind is replaying the way Jake touched me yesterday. The way he kissed my thighs.

That was hot.

Without overthinking it, I grab my phone and snap a photo of my legs with bubbles strategically placed. Just enough to tease, but not too scandalous.

CLAIRE MOORE

Thinking about the way you kissed me here yesterday.

He replies immediately.

JAKE SCHMIDT

You will be my dessert tonight.

Does that mean what I think it does? I hope so. My heart flutters reading that as I watch the typing bubbles appear again, curious what he will say next.

JAKE SCHMIDT

No more screen time.

I giggle, contemplating sending a selfie but settle on a kiss emoji instead.

As the bath cools, I dry off and wrap myself in a robe, craving something hearty for brunch. *Avocado toast with a sunny-side egg and a splash of hot sauce.*

Hot sauce. Samuel. I never ate spicy food before dating him. He loved adding hot sauce to everything, and now ... now it's second nature.

The unspoken rule of our co-parenting arrangement is silence when he has Gabby. No check-ins. No unnecessary texts. But I feel compelled to break it.

CLAIRE MOORE

¿Cómo está mi nena?

How is my baby?
His response is quick.

SAMUEL DÍAZ

Está re bien. Le encanta el agua. Nada un
montón.

*She is doing great. She loves the water. She swims so
much.*

CLAIRE MOORE

Good to hear.

A pause. Then another text.

SAMUEL DÍAZ

¿Ya te está fallando el español?

Is your Spanish already failing you?
I roll my eyes. Is he being an ass? Is this playful? Flirty?
I hope not. Stressed again, I end this conversation.

CLAIRE MOORE

Have her back to my place at 3:00
tomorrow.

No response. Fine. I exhale, turning back to my half-
prepared brunch. *No more distractions.*

I want Jake. I want more time with him. More explo-
ration. More of the way he makes me feel. But am I ready to
let someone in again? A new relationship isn't always going
to be easy, and that scares me. The bad stuff. That's the part
I still don't know if I'm ready for.

26

Jake

At the grocery store, I shop for all the ingredients needed for dinner, but my mind keeps drifting back to Claire. What would it really mean for us to be together? Not just dating, but fully in each other's lives. I tap Nicholas's contact in my phone. He would have some insight into dating a single mom.

"Jake," he answers, warm.

"Hey! Quick question. How long were you and Emily dating before you met her son?"

"Three months."

I reach for a bundle of carrots and frown. *That's a long time.*

"It would have been sooner if it were up to me, but that's what Emily wanted," Nicholas continues. Then he chuckles to himself. "So, you and Claire are hitting it off?"

"Nearly inseparable." I toss a head of garlic into my cart.

"You never know what can bring two people together," he says, seemingly amused. "I like the idea of you two ... but ... she's been through a lot."

"I'm learning." I pause my stride with the grocery cart, considering everything. Claire has enough stress in her life. I can give her peace, safety. I want to give her that. And I'd love to meet her daughter soon. Once we're officially dating, I'll talk to Claire more about that—what she wants from me in that part of her life. I know Gabby has a dad, but I'd still like to be involved—maybe make dinner for the girls once a week or something like that at first.

"Well, I have a lot to do right now," Nicholas says, bringing me back to the moment. "I'll see you both at the barbecue tomorrow?"

"You know it," I say, still thinking about what my life with Claire and Gabby could look like.

⋆⋆⋆

Standing at her doorway with a grocery bag in each hand, Claire greets me with a big smile, messy bun, tank top, and baggy cotton shorts. I lean down to kiss her before stepping in. Placing the bags on the kitchen counter, I ask, "How was your day?"

"Good. Very relaxing." Her eyes dart to the bouquet in one of the bags. "You got me flowers?"

"I did," I say, lifting them from the bag and handing them to her.

"These are beautiful," she says, inhaling the fresh scent, then goes to a cabinet and grabs a vase.

I look around and notice the place looks more organized and put together than yesterday. I spot a photo of Claire and her daughter on the refrigerator. She's precious. Toothy smile, big blue eyes, long hair.

"She looks just like you but with brown hair." Turning to face Claire, I ask, "Where's your slow cooker?"

"I don't have one."

"Really?" I ask, surprised.

"I usually make fast meals." She shrugs.

"Well ... field trip after I put everything in the fridge." I grab the handle, opening the fridge.

"Field trip?" she asks hesitantly.

"We're going to my house to get mine."

She tilts her head. "Why don't we cook at your house then?"

"Nope," I say, shaking my head.

"Why?"

"That wasn't the plan ... and it's your day. When you're tired, you should be steps away from bed."

"I could always sleep in your bed," she tests, moving closer to me and resting her hands on my hips.

My eyebrow raises as I look down at her. "You want to have a sleepover?"

"It's my day right?" she asks, closing the refrigerator door.

"Right ..."

"I want to have a sleepover."

Are we ready to have sex? Am I?

"Claire ..."

"No sex until I'm your girlfriend, I know," she sasses.

"I never said that."

She hums, and I shake my head. "Pack a bag then. For tonight and for the barbecue tomorrow."

She squeals, then skips down the hall. It's cute, and I'm excited to cuddle with her and have her in my bed.

27

Claire

We hop into the truck, and when he presses the button to start it, a band begins playing low. The music is surprisingly good.

"Who is this?" I ask.

"Old Dominion."

"I don't hate *this* country music."

He leans in, cupping my face as he kisses me, his thumb sweeping gently across my cheek before he leans back. "You sure you're relaxed, Sparky?"

I giggle. I guess that was sassy. "This is the most relaxed I've been in years."

He looks over his shoulder, backing out of my driveway, and I notice the Red Lives Matter sticker is no longer there.

"You got rid of the window cling," I say, a bit surprised the only red flag about him is gone.

"I didn't think much of it when one of the guys' wives gave it to us—I saw it as a show of support. But after looking into it more, I get that not everyone sees it that way. I didn't fully consider what I was signaling to the world driving around with it on my truck."

He's too perfect.

I squeeze his hand after he puts the truck in drive. "I like how thoughtful you are." His hand moves to my thigh, his thumb brushing back and forth to the beat of the song as he drives through town. I love the way he touches me.

Taking in his crisp, linen, button-down and shorts, I muse, "You seem to own a lot of linen."

Now I'm self-conscious of my own outfit—drawstring shorts and a tank top.

"Linen is the best. Lightweight, breathable, ideal for summer."

I narrow my eyes, noting the lack of wrinkles. "Did you iron this?"

"I wanted to look nice for you."

"You could have shared the memo." I playfully swat his arm.

"It's your day," he reminds me. "Wear whatever you want."

I laugh softly but am now curious. "And when it's *your* day ... what am I wearing?"

He flashes me a fucking dangerous glance. "Nothing."

Giggling as he turns into a new subdivision, I take in all of the freshly built homes. I don't know why, but it doesn't seem like him. "What made you want to live here?" I ask, staring at the two-story white home.

He presses the button on his visor, and the garage door opens. "I didn't want the maintenance of an old house."

Fair enough.

"This is a big house for a single guy."

"I like to entertain." He reaches for the grocery bags behind us in the cab. I grab my overnight bag and slide out. "And this house will have better resale value down the road," he says, waiting for me in front of the truck.

We step inside, and he moves efficiently, grabbing things from the cupboards. I take a moment to look around. The place is nice—really nice—but so cookie-cutter. It's all white and grey like everything came from the same place. "This feels like an Airbnb," I say, because it looks like a magazine without any personal touches. Not that I can say much since my house doesn't have any personal touches either.

"I'll probably rent it when I'm done here," he says, pulling a cutting board out and reaching for a knife.

"Instead of selling it?" I ask, leaning on the kitchen island, staring at him.

"I am getting into real estate more and more. You can't be a firefighter forever," he easily says.

"Why's that?"

"You never know when your body will start failing you. I want to be prepared, which is why I also bought an apartment investment a couple of years ago."

I consider the pragmatism while watching him wash vegetables. "What's it like being a landlord? Don't people call you all the time?"

"I use a property management company. So, they handle the day-to-day." Jake smiles at me then asks, "Do you want anything to drink?"

"What do you have?" I ask, curious what he keeps in his home.

"Tell me what you want, and I'll let you know if I have it."

"I don't know why but I could go for a gin and tonic."

He hums, bends down, and opens a cupboard. "Gin. Tonic." Then, reaching into the fridge, he pulls out a lime. "You got it."

"Are you going to have one too?"

"Sure."

"I'm not peer-pressuring you, am I?" I giggle, remembering how he said he doesn't drink that much.

He chuckles, pouring the gin into a shaker. "No."

Watching his biceps flex as he shakes the drink, I'm reminded of something else. "Did you forget about the calendar?"

"No." He chuckles again, pouring the drinks into rocks glasses before sliding one across to me. "Cheers, Sparky."

"Cheers, Red." I clink my glass against his.

"We're settled on these nicknames then?"

"Appears so."

A small smirk tugs at Jake's lips as he reaches into one of the grocery bags, taking out the calendar. "For you, Sparky."

A schoolgirl grin takes over my face as I flip through, eager to get to August. When I do, my breath catches.

"Holy shit," I exhale.

Jake, shirtless with suspenders, fire pants, boots, and a helmet. Every inch of him is sculpted and utterly unfair.

"Um, wow," I managed after a few seconds of shameless drooling.

He steps closer, wrapping his arms around my waist. "Should I sign it for you?"

I press my back against him, turned on. I should tell him I want him to recreate the pose instead. But I don't.

"How did you do on the mission?" Jake asks, and I bite back a laugh. He squeezes my hips, turning me to face him. "I hope the girl with the really annoying voice didn't end up with that guy who was into the other girl."

"You were actually watching it?" I giggle. "No, they didn't end up together. But I didn't finish the season. I read after my bath."

"After?"

"Reading before wasn't working. My mind was stuck on everything that's happened these last couple of days." I take a sip of my drink. "Are you serious about coming over and giving me a kiss every night?"

"Why wouldn't I be?" he asks, like I just asked something crazy.

"It's ... a lot."

"How? We live less than ten minutes from each other."

He would be a good boyfriend. Probably a great one. I can't do it though. Not yet anyway.

"My reality kicks back in at three tomorrow when Gabby comes home. So, I want to see how reality treats us before putting a label on this."

"Fair enough. Know that I won't be going out on dates with anyone else."

Looking down at my drink, I consider that. "Well ... same."

He hugs me tight, his warmth surrounding me. "I'm so happy we got to spend this time together. And we still have tonight and tomorrow."

I meet his gaze, a slow smile forming. "It's still my day, right?"

"Right."

"So you're going to make sure I have the best day?"

"I am," he says, his tone slightly wary, probably wondering where I'm going with this.

I slide my hands up his chest, and he sharply inhales. "Then I want you to touch me ... like *touch* me."

28

Jake

"Sparky," I whisper before leaning down to kiss her. Pressing her into the kitchen counter, I deepen the kiss, savoring the way her lips respond to mine. Her blue eyes are hungry, filled with something I want to see more of.

I tug the scrunchie from her bun, letting her hair fall around her face. My fingers trail down her arms, lingering at her wrists. I briefly consider wrapping the scrunchie around them. *Later.* For now, I set it on the counter and slide my hands under her tank top.

"Touch you like this?" I tease, my fingers grazing her skin.

"No."

I smirk as my hands move higher, cupping her breasts. My thumbs brush over the cloth bra, feeling her hard nipples. "Like this?"

"Maybe."

I chuckle, lowering my lips to her neck, placing deliberate kisses along the sensitive skin. She sharply inhales as her body arches toward mine. "Like this?" I murmur against her throat.

She hums, both pleased and frustrated. *I love that sound.*

"Oh," I tease, trailing my fingers lower. "You want me to touch you like this."

When my hand slips beneath her shorts and underwear, she exhales ragged, wrapping her arms around my neck.

"You're perfect," escapes my lips, but I mean it.

She shakes her head, but I don't let her argue, silencing her with a deep kiss. My fingers move in slow circles on her clit, drawing out soft whimpers that only make me want more.

"You are perfect. Look how good you're doing with the eye contact," I praise, then kiss her deep.

"It's not as terrible as I would have thought," she breathes out.

"You like it."

She nods, her cheeks flushed, and I can't wait anymore.

"I think you might like something else."

Dropping to my knees, I slide her shorts and underwear down in one smooth motion.

A breathless laugh escapes her, and I lift one of her legs over my shoulder. Looking up at her, I see nothing but anticipation. I stick out my tongue, teasing, waiting for her approval.

She smiles, nodding.

The moment I make contact, her head tilts back with a sharp exhale.

"Eyes," I command, pulling back just enough to remind her.

She laughs softly, but when her blue eyes meet mine again, I see the need and get to work.

I'm completely lost in her. I want everything she'll give me. I want every sound, every reaction, every part of her.

My tongue moves in slow circles as she grips my hair, her fingers tightening with every movement.

"Fuck," she cries out.

I want to draw this out, to see how many times I can make her come, but she needs to eat dinner. This time, we'll be fast. Later, I'll take my time.

My fingers slide inside her, curling just right, and she gasps.

"Oh my God," she pants.

I tighten my grip on her thigh, anchoring her against me as her body tenses and squirms. I love hearing her breath come in short, shaky bursts.

"Jake," she whimpers, her lids fluttering as she spirals closer.

I watch, completely captivated, until she shatters. I love that she held eye contact as she came. After a final lick, I lower her leg and gently pull her shorts and underwear back up, pressing a lingering kiss to her lips. "I want to do a lot more of that after dinner."

She smirks, eyes still hazy, and I kiss her again.

"Take your drink," I say, brushing my thumb along her cheek, "and recover on the couch."

29

Claire

Oh my God. I can't stop smirking while I sip my gin and tonic and watch Jake prep dinner. This is real. I'm not dreaming. A sexy firefighter is making me dinner after making me come. I giggle, then take another sip.

"What's so funny?" he asks while chopping carrots.

"Our whole meet-cute."

"Meet-cute?" He raises an eyebrow, setting the knife down for a moment.

"Our boy meets girl story."

He nods, looking thoughtful. "It's not every day a sexy woman puts out a fire and then gives me shit about it."

I smile. "So, why did that turn you on?"

"Because I like strong-willed women, and I really like when I make them comfortable enough to be in their feminine energy."

I tilt my head. "Feminine energy?"

"I find the practice of Tantra to be fascinating. I agree with the concept that if I provide stability and structure, then my partner can relax and be fully themselves."

I narrow my eyes playfully. "You keep surprising me."

He chuckles, stepping to the fridge. "Why's that?"

"It's just ... I don't know. It's cool, I guess, that you've put so much thought into this stuff."

"You can thank a couple of my exes," he easily says, now seasoning the chicken. "I didn't seek it out, per se. They were into it, and now I'm really into it." He looks almost bashful after saying that, looking down at the slow cooker for a few seconds. "I don't think we have time for this idea anymore unless you want to have a late dinner."

"Bake it instead?"

He nods and turns to his oven, preheating it and moving the meal to a sheet pan. Washing his hands, he says, "My goal is to always make you feel safe and honored."

"So far so good." I smile, falling for him more and take a sip of my drink.

"You could say this is a flaw of mine," he says, sliding the pan into the oven. "I don't wait for the oven to preheat until I put things in."

"That's a quirk. Not a flaw."

He laughs softly while setting a timer. Jake sinks onto the couch beside me and pulls me close. His arm wraps around my shoulders, and I nestle against him, resting my head on his chest. He takes the drink from my hand and sets it on the coffee table. His fingers tangle in my hair, absently playing with the strands.

"The last two girls I dated were not into the idea of marriage ..." he trails off, and I look up at him. "It's something I would like ... in the future."

"What are you saying?" I ask, barely believing the fact that we are talking about this right now.

He exhales, looking hesitant before finally saying, "If you're dead set on never getting married again, I'll have to start mourning this connection."

I reflexively swat his chest. "Okay, drama queen."

He laughs. "I'm serious, though."

I bite my lip. "I'm not dead set, but I'm also not in any rush." I study his face. "It sounds like you might have some kind of timeline in your head."

"I thought my life would be fully together by thirty-five." He sighs. "But I'm a couple of months away from that birthday, and I still don't have a family."

I soften, my mind wandering to when I decided I needed to get divorced. "Sometimes you have to rewrite the plan." He nods, agreeing. "Why is marriage so important to you?"

"It's serious. It's a commitment stronger than words."

"But the patriarchy of it all ..."

The ownership, like I'm a piece of property. Changing my name again. It was painful enough when I got married, and more painful when I changed it back. All the work I have to do that he wouldn't have to.

He chuckles. "I don't think the patriarchy believes God is a woman, and I do."

"I'm a puddle." I giggle, falling for Jake more and more.

"I don't think the patriarchy wants me to be best friends with my wife either. But I want to be best friends. I want to enjoy spending time with my wife more than anyone else."

He's a dream.

"How does monogamy play into all of this?" I ask because I don't know if Tantra is pro or anti monogamy. Intellectually, I'm against it and have tried being open, but I'm still deciding where I stand on the topic.

"Why are you always looking for some kind of gotcha or flaw with me?"

"It's not that. My ex. He cheated on me a lot. And when

we opened our marriage, he always had a girlfriend. I ... I don't know if I want to share."

"The last girl I dated was bi and poly. It gave me a lot to think about in that way. And I think I want something more traditional."

"Oh?" I giggle, surprised to hear about his last girlfriend.

"Our relationship was more fun than anything. But she'll never be my best friend."

"Fun?"

"The fun you're assuming." He smirks.

"Jake," I whisper, curious.

"But outside of that. The day-to-day monotony wasn't as easy as it is with you."

"Monotony?" I laugh.

"Watching TV, aimlessly driving down country roads ... I'm loving everyday moments with you."

I sit with that for a second, fighting back a smile. Real life. The moments in between. "I wouldn't say my ex and I were best friends." I snuggle into Jake, feeling comfortable in his arms. "We had a passionate connection but lacked the moments in between." My mind drifts back to Jake's last relationship, and my lips twitch with amusement, wanting to know more.

"What?"

"So, you've been with multiple girls at the same time?"

He kisses the top of my head. And the silence is telling me everything I assumed.

"What do you think about winter?" he asks, after a growing pause.

"You're going to talk about the weather now?" I laugh, squirming out of his embrace, needing to see his face. He's blushing.

"Yes. I don't kiss and tell, so let's return to life's more monotonous matters."

What a gentleman.

I shouldn't be smiling this much. "Winter. Like ... the season?"

"Yeah. I've been thinking about traveling more in the winter to make it less terrible."

I breathe into a small laugh as we shift into this mundane topic. "The winter is fine, but the icy roads and snow days are annoying."

He squeezes me tight, bringing me back into his chest. I love these bear hugs. "If we went on a winter vacation, would you rather go skiing or somewhere warm?"

Vacation.

When was the last time I went on vacation? Two years ago. My divorce party, or rather the celebration of me getting a divorce, because it took forever to finalize.

"I like skiing," I share. "I haven't done that in forever."

"Late January, when it's been gray for weeks, we'll go skiing."

"That's cute but—"

"But?" He squeezes me on the couch. "Why are you defensive?"

"I can't just pick up and go. I have to think about Gabby."

"Of course we'll bring Gabby."

My heart nearly skips a beat, and he pushes me back. I flop down onto the couch, and he's hovering above me.

"She'll be at ski school all day. We'll hit the hot tub after a morning on the slopes." His gaze darkens before kissing my neck. "We'll have our time, then pick her up and have dinner together."

I shake my head, trying to bite back a smile. "You make it sound so easy."

His lips tease my collarbone. "It could be." The assuredness on his face. He's serious.

"In January, she'll be five. It seems young for ski school."

"I've seen kids younger out there."

He wants to do this, really do this. "We'll see."

Jake grumbles, then his lips crash into mine. "Right now. I want to *see* how many times I can make you come before dinner's ready."

30

Jake

"I love making you blush like that," I murmur against her lips. I think she's questioning how serious I am, but I am dead set on making her come again and again until dinner is ready.

I kiss down her stomach, then pause, watching her, memorizing this exact moment. The way her body responds to me, the way she looks down at me with that irresistible mix of desire and amusement. I've never wanted someone the way I want Claire. Not just physical, everything. "Keep looking at me while I give you something to blush about."

She smirks. That's another thing I love—when she doesn't shy away from the moment. She's here with me. She trusts me. That's something I don't take lightly.

Claire raises an eyebrow. "You think you can make me come, what, three times?" she asks with some sass in her tone.

Another taunt? Challenge accepted.

"Eight."

Her eyes widen. "Eight?!"

"Did I stutter?"

"I don't know if I've ever gone past four."

I shake my head. "That sounds like a lack of effort on their part."

She giggles, but it's cut short when I press an open-mouthed kiss to the inside of her thigh. I feel her body tense.

"When you squirt," I pause, looking up at her, "then I know I've done my job."

"Jake," she exhales, her voice already wrecked with want.

"Bet you didn't think you would get a pleasure Dom in your meet-cute."

She's trying to fight back a smile, covering her eyes, and her body shakes with laughter.

Smiling, I slide her shorts and underwear off, setting them neatly on the coffee table. I won't be rushed this time. I'll decide when she's ready. I'll take my time, tease out every response, and watch her fall apart for me.

"Take that off," I say, motioning to her tank top. "And the bra."

She hesitates for half a second before slipping them off, revealing herself completely. My pulse kicks up, but I keep my focus on her eyes, making sure she feels beautiful, wanted, safe.

I cup her, pressing the heat of my palm against her. "Tell me you're going to come eight times."

She breathes into a laugh, but I don't let her get away with it. My fingers tighten slightly. "Say it."

"I'm going to come eight times," she says, voice barely above a whisper.

"Good girl."

I flick my tongue over her clit, teasing her, drawing out a shaky gasp. We went too fast last time. This time, I want to figure out exactly what she likes—the pressure, the rhythm, the pace that makes her lose control.

She's it for me.

I know it sounds crazy. I know it's too soon to be thinking about forever, but this is effortless. Claire is the missing piece in my life.

She challenges me. She excites me. She's just starting to let me take care of her, and do I want to take care of her. I want to spoil her, make her feel adored, make her feel worshiped.

I'll wait as long as she needs to be ready to call me her boyfriend.

Hell, she could make me wait years, and I'd still be here. Claire's worth it.

Licking and sucking, I could spend the rest of my life making her feel like this. Making her come undone over and over again, just to watch her body tremble under my touch. I want to learn every inch of her. She deserves that. She deserves everything.

"Fuck," she breathes, and I press my tongue firmer on her. Number one is close. *Should I edge her?* No. I want to get to eight before the timer goes off. I slide in two fingers and begin stroking her walls. "Jake," she pants, breathy and then moans.

I feel her pulsing around my fingers and lift my tongue. Looking up at her, I smile. "One."

I teasingly move my fingers all the way out, then back in. She bites her lip, then flinches when my tongue lands on her. I grab her thighs, holding them in place. I lick slower this time, more delicately.

"Don't squirm away from it," I say, looking back up at her. I release one of her thighs and add my fingers back in.

She tilts her head back, and I'll allow it. I need her to get lost so she can come again.

She breathes, ragged. "I'm close."

I feel it and stay on course, not changing anything. Claire reaches for my hand on her thigh and interlaces her fingers with mine. My heart melts being more connected with her. She squeezes my fingers and then whimpers, shuttering. I kiss up her body, then whisper in her ear. "Two."

"I'm spent," she says, completely limp on the couch.

"No."

She laughs, wrapping her arms around me. "I am."

"Maybe you're scared of what will happen when the next one comes."

"Scared?"

"I know you don't like to be vulnerable. But be vulnerable with me."

She squints at me, and I kiss her deep. "No more wasting time." I kiss her neck and move my kisses down, ready to make number three happen.

31

Claire

"Jake," I hesitantly say, and he looks up, concern flickering in his eyes. "I ..."

I might say something I'm not ready to say if he makes me come again. Fuck him for being so fucking perfect. My chest tightens, and I swallow hard.

"What's wrong?" he asks, crawling back up and hovering above me.

"This is overwhelming."

He softly smiles, then lays next to me, pulling me in to be his little spoon on the couch. "What's coming up for you right now?" he asks over my hair.

"Everything."

He squeezes me tight, resting his head in the crook of my neck. The tenderness takes me over the edge. I feel my throat tighten, and before I can stop it, tears well in my eyes. I quickly wipe them away.

"Baby, look at me."

I hesitate, but I roll over to face him. His hand is gentle as he caresses my jaw.

"Why are you crying?"

"I like you too much," I whisper. "And I'm scared."

Jake brings me in for a hug and doesn't say anything. He just holds me, and that makes me cry even more.

"I don't know if I can handle another heartbreak," I softly say into his chest.

"I won't break your heart." He pushes me back a little, and we're staring into each other's eyes again. He shakes his head slightly, wiping the tears from my face. "I know you've been hurt, but we have to keep living. We learn from our past so we don't repeat history."

I roll my eyes even though it's sweet.

"Claire, I know this is moving fast."

"Why do you want this?"

"Because you are everything I've ever wanted."

I let out a sharp, disbelieving laugh. "You wanted a divorced single mom with a lot of issues?"

His jaw tightens. "Claire. I don't think you have a lot of issues. I know you don't believe me yet, but you're exactly what I've been looking for. Everything about you—the way you challenge me, the way you care so fiercely—it's everything."

I shake my head, trying to push past the lump in my throat. I know he's sincere, but I'm scared to go all in. "I think I should go," I barely say.

"No." Jake pulls me in tight. "You're not running away."

I exhale heavily, but I don't fight him. I don't really want to leave. I just don't know how to stay without completely unraveling in front of him.

We stay like that, silently, cuddled together on his couch, for a long time. My mind won't stop, but my body starts to relax.

The oven beeps, breaking the moment.

"Will you stay for dinner?" he asks, and it sounds like a beg as he cups my face, looking at me so lovingly.

32

Jake

Claire releases me from the hug, and my gut is telling me she is going to leave. But then she exhales softly, as if making peace with something, and says, "I'll stay."

A smile begins to grow on her lips, but mine spreads even faster. Relief floods me. I don't want her to run. Not now. Not ever.

As much as I'd like to dive into the deeper conversations we scratched the surface of, she's fragile right now. I need to tread carefully—keep the mood light while making sure she knows I'm not going anywhere.

"Monotonous dinner conversation?" I joke, trying to lighten the mood.

"I have a few questions I'd like answered," she counters with a sparkle in her eyes.

"Like?"

"You're a pleasure Dom?" She giggles as she says it.

I shrug. "I guess so. I didn't know there was a phrase for it until recently, but yeah." The smirk that follows is too damn cute. I want to kiss it. "Is there a follow-up question, Sparky?"

She leans over to grab her cocktail from the coffee table, taking a long sip. Her eyes flicker with curiosity. "I don't think my follow-up questions would be monotonous, but I'm happy you like to educate yourself."

I wink, then stand, stepping toward the kitchen.

Silence lingers between us as I pull the chicken and vegetables from the oven. I glance back at her. Her underwear is back on. Her fingers are under the band, adjusting it against her hips. *She's so fucking sexy.*

"A pleasure Dom is a first for me," she says, ending my heated stare with her hips.

"We could've eaten naked," I tease, watching her as she finishes dressing.

"Another time. When I haven't been crying."

Claire steps toward me. Her arms slip around my waist from behind. She hugs me, pressing herself into my back. That small act of affection hits me deep.

"Thank you for dealing with me," she whispers.

I drop my hand, covering hers, and squeeze. "You're worth it." That's not a line either. She is worth everything and deserves everything too.

She exhales a laugh. "Famous last words." She gives me a squeeze before pulling away. "Sorry ... I guess I should talk to you about all of the reasons why I am the way I am."

I turn to face her, but she leans against the counter, keeping a small distance between us. I want to tell her she doesn't owe me an explanation. That I'll take her as she is, no conditions. But I also want to know more about what she was crying about.

"My mom and I haven't talked in years, and I never plan on speaking with her again."

"You said she was toxic. How so?"

She shakes her head a little. "The parallels between my mom and my ex—and all my exes—are there. I've done some therapy about it. Probably not enough, but I would categorize them all as narcissistic abuse."

"Give me an example." I don't want to assume, and I'm grateful she is letting me in.

Claire huffs, then reaches for her plate. "This will be our super sexy dinner conversation." Plates in hand, we sit at the dining room table. "My mom, my ex—everyone always had something to say about what I was eating, how much I was eating. I think they wanted me to play a part. The beautiful daughter. The hot wife. Instead of caring about whether I was actually healthy or happy."

My jaw tightens, not liking these assholes. "Is it triggering when I talk about your body?"

"No." She smiles softly. "You talk about it with care. And I know you're not after some specific version of me. I mean, I've been in a ponytail or messy bun and baggy clothes nearly the entire time we've been hanging out. My ex would've told me to put something cuter on or whatever."

I immediately want to tell her how fucking gorgeous she is at all times. Even now as she chews her food. "Can I ask why you cut your mom out?"

She nods, mindlessly spinning her fork. "It was just too much. The constant guilt-tripping, criticism, emotional manipulation ... she was exhausting. When my ex and I started trying for a baby, I thought a lot about the kind of mom I wanted to be. I realized I didn't want to force my child to have a relationship with someone toxic, and that was a big breakthrough. I set boundaries. She didn't respect them. And now, I'm done."

The strength it takes to do that—to walk away from someone who's supposed to love you unconditionally—I can't imagine it. "You're so strong."

She gives a half-hearted shrug. "Ehh."

"You are. Did you do something similar with your ex?"

She huffs a laugh. "Yeah. I was basically a married single mom. Living in a nice, little terrarium. My ex played with us when he wanted to, and when he didn't, he wasn't there. I set rules for how parenting needed to go, and he tried to gaslight me into thinking my expectations were unrealistic." Her fingers tighten around her glass. "I wish I had left sooner."

I want to hold her so badly. "Can I give you a hug?"

She exhales, a small smile playing at her lips. "After dinner."

"You mentioned opening your marriage?"

"If you ever want a fast-track to divorce, open your failing relationship." She cynically chuckles. "It only spotlights the existing problems."

"Did you ever explore?"

"A stay-at-home mom with a baby? With what time?"

I shrug.

"Before Gabby, I had a couple of one-night stands when he was on dates with his girlfriends or whatever. When I was a mom, I never did. Though I did have this flirty thing going with the barista in my building."

I raise an eyebrow. "Did you ever get his number?"

"No. Even though my ex had a girlfriend at the time, I knew he'd feel all sorts of ways if he saw another man texting me. He was more of a 'don't ask, don't tell' kind of guy."

"You're not meaning it like how it means in the military, right?"

"No. He's straight." She shakes her head, pausing. "I need to stop using that phrase."

I nod, agreeing. Glancing at her, searching her face, I refocus the conversation. "What can I do to make you feel less scared ... about us?"

"I think I just need time." She sighs, setting her glass down. "You're annoyingly perfect."

"I'm not perfect." I can be rigid. I shut down sometimes and am overprotective.

"I've been looking for the flaws ..."

"Well, you don't want to do a home project with me, like assembling furniture. I can be intense to work with in that way."

"I wouldn't read the instructions anyway."

I laugh, looking at her empty plate. "Can I hug you now?"

"Yes."

The moment she steps into my arms, I wrap her up, holding her tight. And I know I'll never stop wanting to hold her like this. And I want to keep showing her there is nothing to be scared of with me.

☆
☆
☆

I don't know when we fell asleep, but I know being wrapped up on the couch together is my new favorite hobby. I carried her into bed, and she didn't even stir. Looking at the clock, it's seven in the morning now.

It's probably creepy that I've been staring at her for the last hour, thinking about how much I like her. Considering what our relationship could be.

"Morning," I softly say. She hums like she's not ready to get up for the day. "How do you take your coffee?"

"No latte?" she smiles, her eyes still closed.

"I don't want to leave the house just yet." I pull her into me, nuzzling into her. Last night our bond grew even more. Dinner, conversation, more episodes of the stupid dating show, and endless cuddling.

She rolls to her side, propping her head in her hand. "I don't want to get out of bed."

"We have eight hours left of vacation."

She smirks, then her fingers slip into the waistband of my sweatpants. "Am I ending this vacation without seeing your dick?"

I bite my lip, considering if I should tell her about the gift I got her yesterday. Something I picked up before the grocery store. I roll to face her. "You've done so well with all your missions. Would you like another one?"

"If it involves your dick."

"If you complete the mission, it does."

She licks her lips. "What's the mission?"

"The thing about missions is ... you don't always know what you're getting into."

Claire glares. "Can I have a hint?"

"It involves a toy."

Her head tilts. "A butt plug?"

I laugh deeply. "No."

"Ah—"

"Stop guessing. Say you choose to accept the mission."

I want her to. It will be hot to both be building up the tension and desire all day until it's time for more. I love to play like this and hope she wants it ... but maybe after last night's intensity, she won't be game.

She bites her lip, staring deeply into my eyes. "Okay. I accept."

I smile, leaning down to press a kiss to her forehead. "Let me get coffee going and grab the materials." I slide out of bed. "You need to be showered and dressed before I brief you on the mission."

33

Claire

"Materials?" I cock my head, but Jake just leaves his room with a devilish grin. I make my way to his primary bathroom with my overnight bag in hand and start the shower.

The warm water runs over me, and I think about the shower I took after meeting Jake, after the fire. The emotional release. Now I could nearly cry happy tears. I'm at peace, yet giddy. Our casual evening was perfect, even though it was emotional.

He's perfect.

We've already discussed what this would look like: one date a week, plus a kiss each night. That can work. I want that. I should just do it. Stop being one foot in and one foot out. Dive in.

But what if diving in means drowning?

I flick off the water, pushing the thought aside. I quickly towel off and slide on my summer dress, curiosity about this mission outweighing everything else.

"Beautiful," I hear his voice say and look over seeing Jake leaning on the door frame with two coffee cups in hand. Jake's eyes are glued to me, checking me out as he steps closer. Then a smirk grows on his face as he stands behind me, setting the coffee cups on the counter.

"What?" I ask, watching him in the mirror. His eyes flick between mine, teasing. "What?" I repeat, feeling a heat creep up my neck.

His hands find my thighs, giving them a light squeeze. "I like your curly hair."

"Full glory today."

"When you're done with your hair and makeup, the briefing will take place at the dining room table." He picks up one of the cups and places a kiss on the top of my head. "No rush."

"This is a lot of build-up." *But I'm loving it.*

I quickly get ready, too curious about what's in store for me ... and us. Entering the kitchen, Jake is already seated at the dining table. "When did you shower?" I ask, seeing him now in a polo and khaki shorts.

"A few minutes ago." He gestures toward the small gift bag sitting in front of him. My stomach flutters as I take a seat and reach for it. Opening it, I let out a soft giggle.

"A vibrator for *couples*," I read the packaging, saying "couples" with a questioning edge.

"After today, it might be a little while until I see you again. I thought we could still have some fun together even when I can't see you."

I'm that emoji—the one with the hearts and a smitten smile. He's thoughtful and sweet. My mind drifts to my first mission.

"When did you get this?" I ask, beaming at him.

"Yesterday."

Examining the packaging, I notice there is an app that

controls the device. "Jake," I murmur low, almost breathless. "What is the mission?"

"Building you up at the party."

My breath catches. "You want me to wear it ... *there?*"

"Yes."

I'm not a shy person. But ... we'll be surrounded by my boss, co-workers, and Jake's friends. "That's ..."

"Fucking hot." He winks before squeezing my thigh again. "I want to build you up until I can have you all to myself."

I swallow hard, resting my fingers against my lips, considering the mission.

"Are you going to fuck me later?" I whisper.

Jake smirks. "If you complete the mission."

An excited noise escapes my lips. I'm too excited about everything happening right now and what's ahead. I open the box and giggle, seeing the toy.

"Put it in your purse until we get to the party."

34

Jake

Tapping the address of the party from my text with Nicholas, the directions load, and I punch the gas pedal, the Camaro's engine rumbling in response. Claire smiles bright, and yeah, today is going to be a good day. I like that she's adventurous. I knew she wouldn't hesitate much about the mission, and I love that about her—open, free, willing to play.

It's a short drive to the barbecue, but as we pull through the towering iron gate, we exchange questioning looks. Beyond it stands one of the largest homes on Geneva Lake. It's modern, newer than most of the lake houses, all glass and steel.

"Whose house is this?" Claire breathes in awe.

I shake my head, equally stunned. Nicholas has more money than the rest of our group combined, but he's not flashy. A place like this? It doesn't add up. Unless ... this isn't just a barbecue. *Is he going to propose?* He's had the ring for a while, waiting for the right moment.

As we roll closer, I scan the lineup of cars in the circular driveway—Chad's truck, Chris's minivan, a few others I recognize. The gang's all here. Right on time, as usual.

"Valet?" Claire mutters as a young guy in a crisp, white shirt approaches the car. She arches a brow, giving me a knowing look. "Do you think he's going to propose?"

I shrug, handing over my keys, relieved both of us are dressed nice. The guys make fun of me for how many polos I wear, but they are ready for any occasion.

"I don't know anymore," she says, looking at me with cautious eyes.

I lean in close, brushing my lips to Claire's temple. "Don't know about what?"

"The mission. What if ... it's too naughty."

I steal a quick handful of her ass under her dress, unable to resist.

"Jake!" she scolds in a whisper, her cheeks coloring as she glances around.

"It's up to you how you want to end your vacation."

She hums, trying to fight a smile, but it's already there. Claire interlaces her fingers with mine, and we walk down the hall.

When she points toward a bathroom, releasing my hand, I'm in love. I've been in love, but I fucking love that she is doing this.

"See you outside," I say, my smile showing my excitement.

The expansive patio overlooks Geneva Lake, and the stone pavers look as expensive as this house. I spot Chad and Anna talking to Chris and immediately scan for his wife, Lauren, but don't see her. There is an oversized outdoor sectional with a fire pit, a large yard leading to a beach with Adirondack chairs. The catering spread catches my eye next. A seafood tower? My suspicion grows.

A sudden squeeze on my ass makes me flinch, spinning around to find Claire smiling up at me, her laughter bubbling up.

"Good girl," I say, sliding an arm around her shoulders and dropping a kiss on the top of her head. I love this secret we're sharing.

"An upgrade from Cassandra," Chris says, approaching with a beer in hand. *A little early?* It's barely past ten. He's already drinking? Between the comment about my ex and the beer, irritation flares in my chest.

"Claire, this is Chris," I say, ignoring his comment. "Where's Lauren?"

Chris shrugs. "Couldn't make it."

He's been off lately, and he's not fooling anyone. Chris used to be the guy with the best marriage advice. I need to check in with him later.

"Gotta grab another cold one since no one's here to tell me otherwise," he says before wandering off.

Shaking my head, I look back at Claire. "He's an asshole, but he's our asshole."

She smiles, tilting her head. "Cassandra?"

"The last person I dated."

"Do you have a thing for girls with names starting with 'C'?" she teases.

"Maybe." I pull my phone from my back pocket, opening the vibrator app with a smirk. "Do you really want to fuck around and find out here?"

She bites her lip, and I tap the lowest setting. She flinches, and I bite my lip, loving this.

"That's the lowest setting," I say, my voice low.

"I'll behave," she breathes, but I tap the pulse setting, and she sucks in a sharp breath. "I will!" she squeaks.

"Good girl." I turn it off—for now.

Her chest rises and falls as she steadies herself, biting her lip. It's impossible not to do anything but smirk at her reaction. Before I can say more, I catch Nicholas out of the corner of my eye for a brief moment, stepping onto the patio. A white button down. That's not what Nicholas would wear to a barbecue. This is happening. He's going to propose.

35

Claire

I squeeze Jake's hand, loving this secret game we're playing. "I think you're breaking your rule," I intentionally taunt, because fuck it. I only have a few more hours until reality strikes.

He looks down at me, arching a brow.

"No phones on dates."

He grumbles. "May I have permission to use my phone for one sole purpose on this date?"

"Is that sass?"

He leans down and kisses my neck before whispering, "I will not fuck you here no matter how much you taunt me."

"I need a water." I'm so turned on. "Want one?"

He chuckles, nodding. "I'm going to catch up with Anna and Chad." He gestures toward the server from La Nonna and the guy she's with.

"See you soon." I giggle and step toward the drink troughs on the other side of the patio.

"Taylor, right?" I ask, recognizing the brunette chatting with a guy in front of the water bottles. We had a virtual meeting about encouraging guests to post about High Five on social media.

"Yeah. Claire?"

"Yeah." I look over at the guy next to her.

"Brandon. Brandon Dubois."

Dubois. I wonder if he's related to Kent Dubois. The gallery I used to work at facilitated his four-hundred-million-dollar donation to the Art Institute of Chicago.

Get it, Taylor, I chuckle inwardly, but rich kids are a breed of their own. Is Taylor rich? I have too many nosey questions. But before I can dig into any of them, a sudden pulse between my legs nearly makes me drop the water bottles.

Fuck.

I flinch, too shocked to continue this conversation. Managing a polite "Nice to meet you," I hurry back to Jake.

The moment I'm by his side, I pinch the back of his arm. He wraps an arm around my waist in retaliation, giving my side a playful squeeze. *Jake is fun.*

"This is Claire," he says, introducing me.

Anna waves, and her date extends his hand. "Chad. We met at High Five." I nod, recognizing him now. He's the guy who wore the bunny mask in the bar a couple of months ago, before the fire. "I heard you got to go on the fire boat," he says. "Jake's pulling out all the stops."

"He is." I lean into him, silently praying he will turn this toy off to give me a moment of relief.

"So," Anna says excitedly, glancing around. "This is an engagement party, right?"

We all smirk.

"I'd bet on it," Jake says. "Five bucks that Emily has no idea we are all here."

Chad shakes his head, then confidently says, "This is a wedding."

"What?" we all breathe in unison.

"Look around," Chad says. "You don't have this kind of catering *just* for a proposal."

"No?" Anna asks, raising a brow at him.

He grabs her by the back of her neck, pulling her in for a quick kiss.

"Well, take notes, Chad," she teases, smiling up at him.

They're cute. Even if she is much younger than him. I shouldn't assume every age gap is fucked, but I have to remind myself of that.

"Um," a woman's voice breaks through. She steps closer to us wearing a printed dress with kimono sleeves with a bearded guy in tow. "Did I hear you say you think this is a wedding?"

Chad nods, then asks, "What do you think, Rachel?"

"I *told* you she was being weird," she says, looking up at her date. "I don't know what this is, but it's something big. This is my boyfriend, Patrick, by the way."

"Jake." He extends his hand.

Chad does the same.

"Claire." I wave, recognizing Rachel from High Five— she comes in with Emily sometimes.

"Anna."

"Also, how does Nicholas know Declan Kruk? This is *his* house." Rachel looks at all of us.

Declan Kruk. Another billionaire. My ex used to metaphorically jerk off to that guy and his success, always rambling about how he's the *American dream.*

"Nicholas texted me saying his sister is friends with him," I share.

"Phoenix," Jake mutters, looking around. "I don't see her."

"Have you seen Aaron or Sarah?" Rachel asks.

Our group glances at one another, shaking heads.

"I told you." Chad chuckles. "This is a wedding."

I really hope I'm not wearing a vibrator at my boss's fucking wedding.

36

Jake

Looking around at the guests here, it's obvious everyone senses something big is about to happen, but no one knows exactly what. Would they really have a surprise wedding? I tighten my grip around Claire's waist, eager to find out.

Then, Nicholas steps onto the stone steps leading down to the patio, a glass of champagne in hand. He taps it lightly with a fork, the noise getting the crowd's attention.

The conversations quiet as all eyes turn toward him.

"Alright, alright," Nicholas says, his face beaming with the biggest smile. His free hand rubs the back of his neck like he's nervous having everyone look at him. "I know you're all wondering why we're really here."

A few people chuckle. Chad lets out a whistle, and our group laughs again.

Nicholas smirks, dragging out the silence.

"Well," he says, then takes a slow sip of his drink.

"Tell us!" someone shouts.

He laughs, then looks over his shoulder before looking

at the crowd again. "Let me introduce you to my wife—Mrs. Emily O'Malley."

Holy shit.

The patio erupts in shouts, cheers, and gasps. Everyone is losing their mind. Chad fist-pumps the air. Anna squeals. Claire leans in, looking up at me, wide-eyed and smiling.

Emily steps into the doorway, hand in hand with her son. The crowd loses it all over again as she walks to Nicholas. She's glowing, wearing a fitted white dress with her hair curled.

I glance back to Nicholas. He looks so happy, and that really hits me. I want this moment. I want to share this moment with Claire.

Nicholas takes Emily's free hand in his and leans down to kiss her.

Beside me, Claire wipes a tear from her eye.

"Baby," I whisper, needing to know why she's crying.

She shakes her head, a watery smile breaking through. "This is just ... really beautiful."

The cheers and whistles continue as Nicholas raises his hands, trying to settle the crowd.

"Now that we've gotten that out of the way," he says looking out at the crowd, "welcome to our wedding reception."

The crowd goes wild again, and servers flood out of the home with trays filled with champagne flutes.

I press a kiss to Claire's temple and grab for her hand, interlacing her fingers with mine. Watching Nicholas and Emily walk into the sea of their friends and family, I can't stop thinking about how I want this with Claire.

37

Claire

Taking a sip of the champagne, I can't believe Nicholas and Emily are married. They're perfect for each other, but it's ... making me think of my wedding. I sip, pushing out the memory of four-hundred people watching me walk down the aisle in uncomfortable heels. This is better. Intimate and perfect. And surprising everyone like this? I love it.

"Let's walk down to the lake," Jake whispers in my ear.

His voice pulls me back to the present, and I nod. He takes my hand, weaving us through the crowd and down the steps to the beach. But when my feet meet the sand, I hesitate.

Jake lifts my chin with two fingers. "Are you okay?"

"Yes," I say, although it's a lie.

"Why were you *really* crying?"

I blink a few times. Jake is never going to let me suffer in silence it seems. He's such a great guy.

I exhale slowly, giving in. "My wedding came up ... but that was also a really beautiful and romantic moment we just witnessed."

"I agree. This might be my favorite wedding event I've ever attended."

"Same."

He leans down, pressing a long, deep kiss to my lips. When he pulls back, he chuckles. "I think we need to call off the mission."

I don't want to.

"No."

His brows lift. "No?"

"No."

He scoops me up, spinning me in a circle. "Let's get back in there then," he says, smiling.

Hand in hand, we make our way up the steps to the patio. The hum of laughter, clinking glasses, and music grows with each step.

"Jake," I flirt. "Maybe the mission can move to my place soon."

"Can't hold out?"

I shrug playfully.

"Okay, Sparky." He smirks. "I'll set a timer. Thirty more minutes."

Jake takes out his phone, and my whole body jolts. A sharp vibration pulses between my thighs.

I gasp, eyes wide.

"Oops." His smirk deepens. "Wrong button." Then the sensation shifts to a deliberate pulse. "Now, I'll set the timer."

I glare at him, swatting his arm.

"You think you can last thirty minutes on this setting?"

38

Jake

"This is torture," Claire breathes, and I hear the frustration and amusement in her voice.

"It's called edging," I whisper.

She giggles, bumping her shoulder into mine. "I'm not going to make it."

I swat her ass. "You got this."

"You can't hear it, right?"

I shake my head, enjoying every second of this.

She sharply inhales, squeezing my hand, and I kiss her cheek. I can't wait for what comes after this party. "We need to say congratulations to Emily and Nicholas before we leave." I chuckle, noticing her cheeks are a little pink now.

"No," she says with a breathless laugh.

"Yes."

She whimpers. Actually whimpers. Fuck do I want to leave right now. But this is too fun.

"I could always turn it up more ..."

"No!" She grabs my hand, guiding me toward the happy couple.

"Congrats!" I say, clapping Nicholas on the back, then lean in to hug Emily.

"Thank you." Emily beams, absolutely glowing. But something flickers in my mind when I glance down to see the ring. She doesn't have a champagne flute. *Is this a shotgun wedding?*

I squeeze Nicholas's shoulder slightly, making a mental note to catch up with him soon.

"This was beautiful," Claire says, a little too fast.

Most people wouldn't notice the slight shift in cadence, but I do. The tight breath beneath her words has me holding back a smirk. I press my fingers into the small of her back. *I can't wait to have my hands all over her.*

I pull out my phone to check the timer, but before I even glance at the screen, she snatches it from my hand. She probably thinks I was going to adjust the setting, and I stifle a laugh.

"We have to get going," I say, stuffing down my amusement. "Claire's back to mom duty this afternoon."

"Thank you again for giving me the time off," she says to Nicholas.

He nods and gives my shoulder a squeeze. "Hopefully Jake was good to you."

"Very." Claire exhales, shooting me a mischievous glance.

The heat in her eyes. I won't torture her anymore. "Beautiful day for this. Congrats again."

Nicholas and Emily smile, and I take Claire's hand, ready to go back to her place. The build up all morning has been incredible, and I can't wait to claim her, to give her another reason why we are the perfect match.

39

Claire

S liding into the Camaro, I reach between my legs, ready
to get this vibrator out.

"Did I tell you you could take it out?" Jake asks with a
new authority in his voice.

"Ah–"

His lips crash into mine, cutting me off. It's possessive,
claiming. His hands roam, squeezing my hips, my ass, my
waist—owning every inch of me. "You're wearing it until I
say so."

I moan, turned on and needing more.

He flicks the key, the Camaro rumbling to life as he
pulls down the long driveway. When he shifts gears, I place
my hand on top of his, locking eyes with him. The heated
energy between us is thick.

"Touch yourself," he says, looking over at me. My jaw
drops slightly. His eyes flick down to my thighs before he
looks back at the road. "I want you to come by the time we
get to your place," he says, staring out.

I want to obey, Jake the pleasure Dom.

My thoughts drift to his face between my legs. We're so close to doing that again.

I teasingly glide my hand up my thigh, taking my dress up with it. His eyes flick back to me as I dip my hand beneath my underwear.

"Slow," he commands.

I bite my lip and make soft circles on my clit, teasing myself as the vibrator's pulses build inside me.

"Inhale," he says, his hand resting on my thigh.

He breaks our gaze, looking back at the road. "Exhale."

I release a shaky breath, staring at him even though he isn't looking at me.

"Sexy," he murmurs. "Again."

I take another deep inhale, letting the pleasure rise, my lashes fluttering shut as I surrender to the moment.

"Look at me."

A slow smirk spreads across my lips, but I keep my eyes closed, intentionally disobeying him.

"Fucking look at me."

The car jerks slightly as he unclips my seatbelt. My lids flutter open, confusion flickering across my face—before I gasp.

Jake grabs me, pulling me closer across the bench seat. His hand dives between my legs and tugs the vibrator out. It's quickly replaced by two fingers.

"Oh my God," I pant as he fingers me. "So much for seat belts for safety." I gasp, and he slides his fingers out. "No! Be reckless."

"Buckle up," he commands, putting his hand back on the shifter and staring out at the road. I pout, whimpering, wanting his fingers back inside of me. "Seatbelt." I obey, still pouting. "Now make yourself come."

These commanding phrases shouldn't make me smile

like a fucking schoolgirl, but they do. I bite my tongue and speed up the circles on my clit.

"Good girl."

Staring at him, I can't believe the whirlwind we've had, and I don't want it to stop. I whimper, on the edge as he turns off the main road onto my side street. He flicks his eyes at me, and I'm right there.

Pulling into my driveway, he shuts off the car and leans over, diving his lips into my neck. "Come for me," he breathes into my skin, and I release, shaking as I do. "We're getting to eight this time," he grumbles, holding my gaze, then leans down farther to pick up the toy from the floor.

40

Jake

When she shuts her door, I flick the lock and reach for her hips, pushing her toward the kitchen sink. My lips crash into hers as we make our way there. Dropping the toy in the sink, I consider how we have two hours to play. Plenty of time.

One down, seven to go.

"Get naked. The next two hours are mine."

"Yours?"

"Mine."

She grabs for the hem of her dress and glides it off.

"Your skin is beautiful, Casper." I tease, placing small kiss after small kiss on her pale chest. She giggles, reaching behind her back and unclasping her bra. I catch the strap and toss it across the room as my lips move up to her neck. I shove her down on the bed and grab for her underwear, tugging it off. I drop to my knees, pulling her to the end of the bed and into my face.

I've craved her all fucking day.

When my tongue lands on her, I moan. Could she be any more fucking wet for me? I lick and suck, not wanting to take my time. I need to be inside her after this orgasm. I flick my eyes up and find hers already staring down at me.

She's perfect for me.

I press harder with my tongue and slide two fingers deep. She cries out, and I reach for her hand, interlacing our fingers. She squeezes mine tight. Her hips rock on my face, and I keep at it, needing to feel her shatter.

"You're so good at this," she pants.

I tap my tongue on her clit in a fast rhythm, and she bites her lip while her body starts to tremble. I go back to making firm circles.

"Yes," she whimpers.

I pound my fingers harder until her whole body shutters. Feeling the pulses of her orgasm, I keep my tongue on her, flicking ever so slowly as my fingers stay inside. After savoring her release, I move my lips to her thighs before kissing her body.

"What do you think about three?" I ask, checking in.

"Yes, please."

"So polite," I tease, grateful she wants to keep going because I do not want to stop now. I fucking love making her come. "Would you like it from my cock?"

She nods, and I lean back on my knees and toss my shirt off. Taking my wallet out of my back pocket, I set it on the bed, then stand, taking off my shorts and briefs. She hums, approving, and I smirk. I can't wait to feel her like this. Picking up my wallet, I open it to take out the condom I put there this morning.

I tilt my chin. "Get yourself to the top of the bed."

She rolls over, crawling up, and I can't believe how quiet she's being. "Sparky," I say, needing to check in again. "Are you doing good?"

"Very," she says, sexy as ever.

"You're so quiet."

"I'm being a good Sub for you," she says with a light laugh.

I grumble, mentally noting to talk more about that later. But not right now. I'm loving everything about this moment, today, the days we've shared. "What do you think about being a good girlfriend for me?"

"Let's see how *good* this dick is."

I huff, loving her taunts. Opening the condom wrapper, I slide it on, staring at her as I do, ready to make her mine.

41

Claire

Jake the multihyphenate fucking dream is about to break my back with his monster cock and make me his girlfriend. Life is good. No. Life is great.

Best vacation ever.

Positioned between my legs, he's looking down at me like I'm the most beautiful woman in the world.

"You can close your eyes if you want." He gives my knees a squeeze, and a soft smile grows on his lips.

"Already making concessions in our relationship?"

He leans down and presses a kiss to my neck, then kisses up to my ear. "Good girls get rewarded."

I giggle, ready for this.

He leans back and palms his cock. "I want to go slow."

"Okay," I whisper, excited.

"Ready?"

"Yes."

I breathe out as he enters me. *Ah.* He's thick. All the way in, he closes his eyes like he's savoring the moment. His lids flutter open, and he confesses, "You're my dream girl."

Internally melting, he's my dream guy too. Well, the

new version of my dream guy. What I should have been envisioning all along.

"So tight," he grumbles. Jake hovers over me and leans down for a kiss. He's barely thrusting as he tenderly kisses me. *Slow.* We're going slow. I like slow, and wrap my arms around his neck, not wanting to ever stop kissing him. He bites my bottom lip, and my hips rock in response. Our eyes are searching each other, silently communicating.

"I'll have you on all fours after this," he says, and I smirk, loving how he can read my mind sometimes. "You're going to have your hair in a ponytail too."

I giggle, and he leans back, his hand running down my chest and stomach, landing on my clit. "I love watching you come." His thumb presses just right, building me up as his cock teasingly thrusts. Then, his rhythm changes. He's going nearly all the way out before pumping back in. "You're a goddess."

I pull him down to me, needing to kiss him again. He felt too far away on his knees, and I need to be close, as close as we can be. His tongue swipes across mine, and I think about how much I love his tongue. The way it spoils me. My hips rock again, getting close with his fingers and cock at work.

His chest rumbles. "You're so tight." His hand cups my neck, his thumb teasing the skin. "Do you want to close your eyes?"

"No."

He bites his lip, his hand squeezing my neck the slightest amount. "You're so fucking perfect."

Removing his thumb from my clit, he props himself over me and fucks me harder. His thrusts are hard, but slow. He stares deeply into my eyes before squeezing my neck for a moment then releasing it. Propped up on both hands, he thrusts hard and fast, staring down at me, and all I can think about is werewolf romance and imprinting. This is the closest I've ever been to feeling like my soul is merging with another.

He smirks. "Sparky, stay in this moment."

I grab the back of his neck, bringing him down for a kiss and rock my hip to the side. I want to be on top. He picks up my cue, and I roll on top of him, staying inside.

He hums, looking up at me, and his thumb goes back to my clit. "This is how you're going to come."

I roll my hips in a circle over and over feeling him in a new way.

Great cock.

Another point for the perfect guy. He thrusts up, and I squeak, not expecting that.

"Lean back," he commands. "Rest your hands on my thighs."

I lean back and instinctively close my eyes, giving in to all of the sensations. He slowly thrusts up, and it feels like the toy pulses from earlier. The circles he's making with his thumb speed up.

I want to come. I want to feel his cock in me as I shatter. I open my eyes, wanting to see him most of all. My orgasm crashes through me, and I flop down on him. He holds me tight as the waves of it run through me. My eyes go wide as I feel his dick throb inside of me. I look up at him from his chest, and he smiles, running his hand through my hair. Wordlessly conveying so much.

42

Jake

Playing with her hair, I want to spend the rest of my life doing this over and over again. Fuck that was perfect. "Where do you keep your scrunchies?" I ask, nearly recovered.

"The first drawer on the right in my bathroom."

"What about another condom?"

Her brows knit together. "You don't have to—"

"Today. Yes."

She rolls off my chest and pulls open the drawer of her nightstand. "Here." She hands me another condom.

"I'm going to the bathroom," I say, setting the condom on the nightstand. "When I get back, you better be on all fours."

"Oh yeah?" she asks with a bratty edge in her tone.

I roll on top of her, pinning her arms down. "You can always fuck around and find out."

She hums, like she's deciding what she's going to do. I release her wrists and slide out of bed. Looking over my shoulder, I remind, "All fours."

In her adjoining bathroom, I roll the condom off and

toss it in the trash. Taking a piss, I look up at the ceiling. I hadn't imagined meeting my wife on the job.

Wife. I've never thought about anyone else like that. But it feels right.

Washing my hands, the anticipation of how I'll find Claire grows. Will she be a brat or not? Either way, we'll have fun. Opening the scrunchie drawer, it's nearly overflowing. I finger through and find a patriotic one with stars and stripes. Perfect.

Stepping back into her room, she's on all fours, and I smile.

"Took you long enough," she says over her shoulder.

I grumble. "That mouth of yours." Standing at the side of the bed, I squeeze her ass. "Maybe I should punish it ..."

She licks her lips, holding my gaze, and my cock twitches, ready for more.

"Show me what else that mouth is good at."

Claire crawls to me. Staying on all fours, she reaches for my cock, stroking it before taking it into her mouth. My head tilts back as she sucks and licks.

"That's it."

I gather her hair and smirk, since I'm still holding the scrunchie, and tie it into a ponytail. She giggles while sucking, and I love it. I wrap her hair around my fingers and begin guiding her, taking control. With each bob, I'm surer of all of the feelings I have for her.

"I love this fucking mouth."

As much as I like this, I don't want to come yet. I tilt her chin up by pulling her hair. "Go face the headboard."

She releases me and gets into position. I grab for the condom, taking all of her in as I unwrap it and roll it on. "I'm not going slow this time."

"Break my back," she demands.

I chuckle. "You asked for it." I yank her hips back slightly. "Stay like this."

Palming my cock, I guide myself in, exhaling as I do. All the way in, I squeeze her hips, thrusting hard. Her head drops as she moans. Fuck. I thrust faster.

Grabbing her ponytail, I pull her head all the way back and whisper, "You take it so well." I release my grip on her hair and thrust deep. The sounds she's making. I love them. I push her back down into the bed so her chest rests on the covers while her hips are high. I run my hand down her back, and she turns her cheek to the side, resting it on the bed.

"So fucking sexy, Claire." I collect her wrists and bring them behind her back. With my other hand, I yank out the scrunchie and wrap it around her wrists. "Stay like this."

Squeezing her hips, I thrust hard and fast.

"Jake," she pants.

"Harder or softer?"

"Harder."

I bite my lip. "Faster or slower?"

"Faster."

"You got it," I huff, nearing a sweat as I fuck her. Railing her with everything I have, her noises and the sound of her ass slapping into me are quickly bringing me to my release.

Honest noises are the sexiest sounds.

I dig my hands into her hair, pulling it as I lean down to whisper, "Be a good girl and come on my cock."

I release her hair and slide my hand under her, circling her clit with two fingers. I slow my thrusts, wanting her to come. "Come for me," I demand.

With each pant, I know she's almost there as I lazily fuck her. My fingers have her on the edge. "Right the fuck now, Claire."

She whimpers the sexiest noise, and I feel her quaking around me. I lift my fingers and trail them along her body until I squeeze her ass. Playfully swatting it, I taunt, "Four."

I pull out and flip her onto her back. "Time for five." I grab her legs, placing them over my shoulders and re-enter. Fucking her hard, I tap my thumb on her clit in motion with my thrusts for added sensation. "I need you to give this to me," I say, strained, nearing my own release.

Her eyes flutter shut, and her hand bumps my thumb out of the way. She makes fast circles on her clit while I relentlessly rail her.

"Fuck," I huff, coming without notice. Euphoric, I feel my cock throb. As much as I'd like to flop on the bed and hold her into me, we're not done yet.

I want five. I want to make her come more than anyone else ever has.

I pull out and bury my face between her legs, needing this orgasm from her. "Jake," she squeaks, surprised. I grab for her hand, interlacing her fingers with mine as I feather my tongue on her clit, staring up at her.

"This one is going to kill me," she pants.

I add a finger, circling inside of her while I focus my attention on her clit.

"Fuck you," she says, breathlessly.

I chuckle, loving it.

"I'm close."

I need this. I squeeze her hand tight, wanting to signal it's time. Her body tenses, and she squeezes my hand, holding it tight as she whimpers over and over. Her body convulses, and she releases her grip on my hand.

I kiss the inside of her thigh, then hover above her. "Five."

She softly laughs, and I flop down next to her. Claire

snuggles into my chest, and I wrap my arm around her, holding her close. Mindlessly playing with her hair, staring at the ceiling, my mind won't stop repeating: I love her.

The sound of a snore brings me back. I smile, looking down, seeing she's asleep.

We're going to have to work on her stamina.

I turn my head to her clock. I'll wake her in twenty minutes. Her vacation is almost over, and I can't wait to see what our real life will look like.

43

Claire

Hard knocking sounds jolt me awake. I roll out of Jake's arms, and my eyes dart to the clock. 3:07 p.m. "Fuck!" Gabby is back with her dad.

I scramble to my feet, tugging on my shorts. "Jake! Wake up." I frantically get dressed and sweep my hair over one shoulder, desperate to smooth it into something less obvious. "Stay in here," I whisper, already moving toward the door.

He nods, but I catch the flicker of emotions running across his face.

This is not how this was supposed to happen.

I crack open the door, and before I can say a word, Gabby barrels into me, wrapping her arms around my waist. I bend down, holding her tight, but my pulse is racing.

This is the worst possible scenario. It's too soon for my ex and Gabby to meet Jake.

I manage to keep my voice light when I ask, "¿La pasaste bien el fin de semana, mi amor?" *Did you have a good time this weekend, my love?*

"Sí, mamá!"

"Did you buy a car?" Samuel asks, and my heart sinks. Jake's Camaro is parked in the driveway. Before I can say anything, I notice Samuel has a bouquet of flowers in hand. Flowers?

What the fuck?! I might pass out at everything going on right now.

Samuel's entire demeanor shifts. His head tilts slightly, then squints. "Is there a guy here?"

"What?" I breathe.

His eyes drag over me, intently. "Your hair only looks like that after ..." He trails off, his jaw clenching.

Heat floods my face. I shouldn't feel shame. I am a grown woman. I can sleep with whoever I want. But there's something about him standing there, watching, analyzing, calculating that brings this feeling to the surface.

He turns to Gabby, asking her in Spanish, "¿Conociste al novio de mamá?" *Have you met Mommy's boyfriend?*

Gabby giggles and shakes her head. "Mommy doesn't have friends."

A bitter laugh escapes me as my stress continues to grow.

"If there is a guy here, I need to meet him," he says coldly.

"No."

His eyes narrow, and he switches to Spanish. "En la casa donde está mi hija, sí." *In the house where my daughter is, yes."*

"No."

This hypocritical bullshit. Gabby has met so many women whose names I don't even know and will never know. The precedent has long been set–by him.

"So, there *is* a guy here?"

I take a steady breath, forcing myself to stay calm.

"Gabby, can you play in the living room while your dad and I talk?"

She skips away, and the second she's out of earshot, I turn to him. "Samuel, don't be a dick."

"Always the victim."

My fists clench and I bite back, *Always the gaslighter.*

"Why were you texting me if you have a guy?"

I scoff, stunned. "You think me asking how my daughter was doing was me *flirting* with you?"

The familiar cocky expression crossing his face makes me want to scream.

"Is he hiding in your bedroom?"

Frustration boils, and I manage, "Please leave."

"I'm not leaving until I know who is in this house."

"It's not your right to know."

"My daughter is here, and I pay the rent. It is my right." He steps farther into the home.

"Leave!" I yell.

Samuel doesn't turn away. He pushes past me, dropping the flowers onto the kitchen island. My body stiffens as he walks down the hall.

Jake emerges from my room, dressed. Thank God. Samuel stops and shakes his head before he looks back at me muttering, "Puta."

Fucking hypocrite.

"Háblale con más respeto en su casa," Jake says, and I blink hearing him tell Samuel to speak to me with more respect in Spanish. There is too much going on to process that Jake seems to know Spanish.

"*Mi* casa."

I groan. Samuel is being a fucking asshole. "You need to leave," I assert, hoping this testosterone-laced tension doesn't boil over.

The last fucking thing I need today is them throwing fists. They silently stare at each other for a few seconds until Samuel turns and walks past me. He stops in the living room doorway.

"Gabby, hug," he calls, bending down to scoop her into his arms. Then, he looks directly at me. "Do you want to spend more time in Chicago?" he asks her.

"Yeah!" She squeezes him.

His gaze stays on me. "I want you to spend more time with me."

I hate him, and all of the implications that can be drawn from his words. I'm on the verge of tears, overwhelmed by everything going on. When the door shuts, Jake is behind me, grabbing for my hand. I pull away.

"You need to leave too," I snap.

"Claire ..."

"Leave."

"Baby." He reaches for my hands.

I rip my hands away, throwing them in the air. "Fucking leave."

His jaw tightens. I see his chest rise and fall as he scans my face, too deeply, too searchingly. "I'll call you later," he tentatively says.

"No."

"Claire ..." His voice is heavy with something I can't handle right now.

My tears begin to fall, too many emotions are rising to the surface, especially my fear of losing Gabby. "I told you this wasn't going to work," I say tightly, pushing Jake to the door.

44

Jake

Sitting in my car, I don't want to leave. Every part of me wants to turn around, knock on her door, and tell her she doesn't have to deal with everything alone. That she never has to be alone again.

I let out a long breath, pressing my forehead against the steering wheel. My fingers drum against the leather as I replay everything. I should have set an alarm. I can't believe I fell asleep too. I should have been up, dressed, already out of the house long before three. I should have been prepared. But I wasn't. And now ... I wipe a tear from my eye. This can't be over.

It physically hurts thinking about never seeing her again. Never touching her. Never getting the chance to prove to her that I'm not like him.

Every instinct I have is telling me to fix this, to fight for her—but she's not ready. Pushing her right now would only drive her further away.

She's too triggered from her ex. And I fucking hate that he still has that power over her. I hope there isn't any merit to his words, and I really hope my being there doesn't give him added ammunition to push for more time with Gabby.

"Fuck," I breathe out, tapping my head on the steering wheel.

Sitting in silence, one thought is louder than the rest: I need to give her space. Even if it kills me. Even if it means stepping back when every part of me is screaming to step forward. Because if I push her now, I might lose her forever. And that's a risk I can't take.

45

Claire

Holding back every emotion, I reach for the remote and turn on Gabby's favorite movie.

"I'll make popcorn," I manage, my mind racing with questions. I need to call my lawyer. *What could Samuel do?*

Gabby climbs into the couch, and I wrap her in a blanket, adding some of her favorite stuffed animals.

"The bear." She points to the stuffed bear Jake gave her. I grab it. Tears spill down my face before I can stop them. I hand it to her quickly, blinking hard, swallowing the ache in my throat.

I throw Samuel's flowers in the trash and then look at the ones Jake got me. I yank them out of the vase, getting rid of them too. I toss the popcorn bag in the microwave, and my eyes drift to the toy in the sink. I huff, walking away to get my phone. Stepping into the bathroom, I need a moment alone. The second the door shuts, I dial my attorney.

I don't think anything that just happened could change my custody agreement, and I need to confirm. It goes to voicemail, and I manage, "I need to talk."

I won't put anything in writing. I won't leave a trail. I've learned that much through this whole divorce and custody battle. But I want to. I want to text Samuel and tell him exactly how much I hate him. How much I hate what he does to me.

Tears fall fast, and I resist the urge to throw my phone. My vacation from reality is over. No more breathing room. No more stolen time. Back to reality. Our reality: me and Gabby. That's all I can handle.

46

Jake

I pull back the blankets, but I don't get in. I'm tired from the long day, but my mind won't quit. My bed feels empty without her. I stare at my phone, thumb hovering over the screen.

There's too much to say. I want to call her. Hear her voice. Fix this. But it's 8:30 p.m. and her daughter's likely asleep. Claire could be asleep. As much as I want to call her, a call might feel like too much. I'll just send a text.

JAKE SCHMIDT

I'm sorry I didn't set an alarm. Can I come over tomorrow night after Gabby is asleep so we can talk?

47

Claire

I blankly stare at my phone, and tears drip down my face. *No.* I knew this wasn't going to work. Now it's all fucked. I can only imagine what power move Samuel will play, and I can't take it, any of it.

I'm better off alone.

✩
✩
✩

Tucking the blanket around Gabby, my phone buzzes on her dresser. *Please be my lawyer.*

I place a goodnight kiss on Gabby's cheek as she nestles into her pillow. "Te amo. Buenas noches." *I love you. Good night.*

"Te amo," she softly says back.

I grab for my phone, seeing a missed call from my lawyer. *Samuel is not getting more custody of her.* I'll do whatever it takes to make sure that doesn't happen. Shutting Gabby's bedroom door softly, I tap the missed call and lift the phone to my ear.

"What's going on?" Andrea asks immediately.

"I'm freaking out. Samuel said some loaded things when he dropped off Gabby today."

"What happened?"

Pacing in my bedroom, I give her a play-by-play of every second of the exchange and wait for her to respond.

"You're dating." Her tone is factual, not unkind, just straightforward.

I was dating. I nearly correct her—past tense. But instead, I bite my cuticle and stay quiet.

"Samuel hasn't experienced that yet." She pauses. "Of course, his narcissistic ass is upset by that."

I let out a small, bitter laugh. Then ask what's really weighing on me. "What are the chances of him being able to modify the agreement?"

"Low."

My shoulders drop, feeling immediately relieved.

"He'd have to prove that there's something unsafe or harmful about Gabby being with you. Simply having a boyfriend—even if he spends the night—doesn't meet that threshold ... unless this guy has something in his past."

Jake? No. But also I don't fucking know. I barely know him. My stress rises again as I consider what to say.

"You're entitled to live your life, Claire," Andrea says into the silence.

"But ..." I start pacing again, considering how Samuel is. "What if he tries to weaponize it? He can afford to drag me into court whenever he wants to."

"Money doesn't equal custody."

She's right, but spending money I don't have to fight him ... I loudly sigh, trying to relieve the stress.

"Does he actually want more time with Gabby?" she asks, her tone more of a statement than question. "No."

I press my lips together, nodding. *He only cares about winning.*

"He has no case, Claire," Andrea continues. "But I need you to stay diligent about keeping records."

"Okay."

"Any aggressive texts. Any time he makes a comment that feels like a manipulation tactic. Log when he's late for pickups or misses a weekend with her. If we need to use it, then we will be able to prove he's inconsistent as a parent."

"I'm so tired of fighting him," I barely say, thinking back to how we got here, to our current custody agreement.

"I know. If he escalates, we're ready."

I pinch the bridge of my nose, nodding even though she can't see me. "Thank you."

"Of course. You know I love fucking entitled men in court, but let's hope it doesn't get there. You need to stay mature, grounded, level headed. We are here to win the war, not each battle." She softens. "And you're not doing this alone. You have me on your side."

Alone. The word repeats in my mind, Jake's face appearing. He stood up for me. He would fight for me in a second, and I still pushed him out the door. I'm not ready.

I don't want to be a damsel in distress. Jake already puts out enough fires, and I can fight my own battles. Most importantly, I need to focus on Gabby.

48

Jake

Monday, July 7th

At the station, my mind is anywhere but present. It keeps replaying what happened yesterday. What could I have done better? What should I have done? What can I do now?

My phone vibrates in my pocket, and a smile grows on my face, hoping it's Claire calling me back. Seeing the name on my screen, it's not hers. It's my brother, Jeremy, and I tap to answer.

"Hey, sorry to call you while you're at the station," he says.

"It's slow. All good."

"What did I do?"

"What do you mean?" I ask, unsure of his tone.

"Usually you keep me up to date about girls, and Mom called saying you found *the one*."

I shake my head. "It's complicated." I sigh, still unsure what I should do about yesterday.

"How so?"

"She isn't talking to me at the moment."

"What did *you* do?"

I loudly exhale, reliving yesterday afternoon. "Her ex is a dick. And she's scared of letting someone in now."

Jeremy hums. "If she's the one. It will work itself out."

"I wish I knew what to do," I say, running my hand through my hair. "My gut is telling me that if I do something it's only going to push her away."

"Trust your gut. It's never failed you."

I shake off a memory from Iran, telling my guys to turn around. I don't want to think about how our tank was the only one that made it through that day.

"Look how long Tess and I dated long distance before the stars aligned," he says into the silence. "Be patient."

Years. I don't want to wait years, but who knows how Claire feels at this point? I consider his relationship for a moment, then confess, "Patience is hard."

"You don't have to tell me. No one believed me when I said I found love at a Vegas pool party. But here we are. Expecting."

"What?!"

"Yeah. That's really why I called."

"Congrats!"

Shit. I need to check in with Nicolas and Chris. I've been so lost in my thoughts about Claire since she kicked me out of her house.

Two weeks later
Sunday, July 20th

It's safe to say she ghosted me. My last two calls went straight to voicemail. No texts. Just silence.

I know she's scared—scared of something real, scared of

what this means for her life, scared of the drama with her ex. At least that's what I'm telling myself. Because if I let myself believe she didn't feel the same way, I don't know how I'll handle that. The time we spent together was life changing, and I don't want to imagine never seeing her again.

I'm desperate at this point. I've thought about showing up at High Five. I've thought about leaving her notes on her front step. I don't want to push her further away, but I also don't know how to let go.

Frustrated, I pull into the grocery store, hoping the routine of picking up my essentials will get her out of my mind for a few minutes. Pushing my cart, I nod at the familiar faces. I rarely buy cookies, but I feel like eating my feelings today. Turning my cart into the aisle, I spot Claire and Gabby. A smile immediately grows as my heart starts to race.

We were bound to run into each other at some point.

"Claire," I call out, and she looks over. She smiles, but then it looks like she is tightening her face trying to hide it. "How are you?"

"Fine." Her tone is tight, but her eyes flick down my body.

I'll call that progress.

I turn to Gabby, my voice lighter. "Which cookies are your favorite?"

"These!" she squeals and points to a brightly wrapped package. *She's cute.*

"Those look good. I'm hoping they will make me feel better," I say, grabbing the pack.

Gabby also takes a package from the shelf and drops them in their cart. Claire groans, and I see how that situation isn't great. "Let me get them," I say, opening my wallet.

"No."

I grumble, then an idea strikes. I remove the cookies from their cart and look at Gabby, then at Claire. I want to spend time with them. "I'd love to have you both over before these expire. I can make dinner, and we can have these for dessert."

Gabby smiles, then looks at her mom.

"Maybe," Claire says.

Maybe. That's actual progress. I celebrate by overtly checking her out.

Before I can stop myself, I say, "If you ever need help completing a mission, call me."

The tight smile on her lips. There were two opportunities for her to say no, and she didn't. Yeah, I'll take that progress.

49

Claire

"Claire," I hear Jake's voice and turn, spotting him a few steps away from us in the aisle. I should have known this would happen eventually, running into him. Lake Geneva is small. *Why does he have to look so good in this green polo and black shorts?* I hold back a smile, thinking about how he is always put together.

I feel terrible about ghosting him. Hiding felt safe—until now.

"How are you?" he asks.

"Fine," I say quickly. I'm not hashing this out in a grocery store aisle with Gabby next to me. If Jake wasn't so attractive, if he wasn't perfect, maybe this would be easier.

"Which cookies are your favorite?" he asks Gabby.

"These!" she squeals and points to the animal sugar cookies.

Jake reaches for a pack, tossing it into his cart. "Those look good. I'm hoping they will make me feel better."

I fight back a smirk. I guess we've both been eating our feelings, then. I've been doing it with frozen chocolate-covered strawberries.

Gabby pulls a package from the shelf and drops it in our cart. I groan. We already have too much junk food.

"Let me get them," Jake says, reaching for his back pocket and opening his wallet.

"No," I snap. Then scold myself for the reaction. He is being nice. He is being the perfect fucking gentleman that he always is.

Your bullshit is keeping you from having this great guy.

Jake steps closer, taking the cookies out of our cart. He looks down at Gabby, then at me. "I'd love to have you both over before these expire. I can make dinner, and we can have these for dessert."

I could groan again at how perfect he's being, even though I've been an asshole to him.

Gabby's eyes are looking up at me, smiling.

"Maybe," I breathe.

Jake's eyes slowly rake down my body. My mind flashes back to him taking me, absolutely railing me. It was so fucking good.

"If you ever need help completing a mission, call me."

I nearly flinch, my mind replaying him teasing me with the toy. I force myself not to smile. And I fight back the urge to jump into his arms and make out with him. I need to start up therapy again. I don't want to fuck this up, and I'm not ready for the love he is offering me.

50

Jake

Twelve days later
Friday, August 1st

C had is cleaning us out tonight. I comb my hands through my hair, exhaling as he flops down a straight on his dining room table in his backwoods cabin. We all shake our heads, and he drags the pot of chips toward him.

"You aren't supposed to win in your own house," Chris grumbles, tossing his cards down.

"You stacking the deck?" I joke.

"I feel like I'm the only one concentrating on the game," Chad says, sipping his beer.

He isn't wrong. Nicholas keeps turning his wedding band on his finger. I wonder if he's told the other guys yet. Chris is downing beer like it'll drown out his separation, and I ... I'm thinking about Claire.

I know she wanted space. I told myself I'd respect that.

But all night, my mind's been looping back to her. To the way she looked at me in the grocery store. The way she didn't tell me to fuck off when I invited her over. The way she reacted when I mentioned the mission.

Should I just give up on the idea of us? I don't want to. I've given her space, but maybe too much. Maybe I should be bold, do something—

My phone buzzes on the table.

CLAIRE MOORE

I would like another mission.

I blink. That can't be real. Swiping open my phone, my lips curve into a smirk. My pulse kicks up, my whole body reacting to this, to her. I stand, needing a minute alone.

"Taking a piss," I mutter, heading to the bathroom.

A mission. What would be just enough to thaw the ice but not too much? Does she still have the toy? I still have the app.

Should I call her? Would that be too much? Or would it be exactly what we both need?

She texted. We'll text.

JAKE SCHMIDT

When it's in, I'll give you directives.

I hope she didn't throw away the toy.

CLAIRE MOORE

In.

Fuck. I rub my forehead, exhaling slowly. Her keeping the toy is giving me too much hope right now. I bite my lip, considering what I should say.

JAKE SCHMIDT

Touch your body. Think about the way I touch you. I'll turn the toy on soon.

I imagine her doing exactly that. I wish I could be there next to her. Exhaling sharply, I push my phone back in my pocket.

Rejoining the guys, I clap Chad on the shoulder. "Thanks for taking all my money. I'm calling it a night."

"Come on, it's early," Chris pouts.

Nicholas holds my gaze for a moment, then a playful smile breaks across his face. "Have fun."

I shake my head but don't respond. I turn toward the door before anyone can start asking questions.

Sitting in my truck, I stare at the app, considering what I should do. The eight-minute drive home is going to feel like an eternity, but I can't sit in Chad's driveway all night. I hit the lowest pulse setting, then text Claire.

JAKE SCHMIDT

Call me to continue the mission.

Down the country road, my phone stays dark. Nothing.

Maybe she just wants it to be sex.

Maybe a call is too personal.

Maybe she isn't ready, and I was getting my hopes up for nothing.

Disappointment takes hold until the screen lights up the cab. I don't even hesitate, tapping the answer button.

"Hey," I probably sound winded. My heart is nearly beating through my chest because I've missed her.

"Hi," she says softly, and fuck, I've missed her voice.

Silence hangs between us. I remind myself she isn't calling to catch up.

"Do you want a quick mission or a long one?" I ask, wanting to keep her on this call as long as possible though.

"Depends."

"On?"

197

"If ... I mean ... whatever you think I deserve for being an ass."

I shake my head, smirking. "You're not an ass."

A small pause. "I am."

I put my phone on speaker, quickly reopening the app and increase the intensity. She breathes, ragged. "Tonight's mission will be a little different."

"Yeah?" she pants.

I think she's looking for a punishment.

"You're not going to come until I tell you to. No matter how good it feels or how long I play with you."

"Okay," she pants.

"You'll have to suffer through this intensity until I get home. It will be a few more minutes."

She hums. I fucking want to go to her place. To hold her. To kiss her.

Don't push too fast.

Hearing her breathe, I smile. "Deeper inhales, baby."

"I've missed you," she whispers.

My heart pounds hearing that. "I've missed you too."

I rub my eyes, fighting back happy tears. Our story isn't over. I swipe back into the app and change the intensity back to its lowest setting.

"Why did you text me tonight?"

"It's August."

I knit my brows together, not understanding.

It's silent until she says, "The calendar."

I chuckle, having almost forgotten about the department calendar. "Are you looking at it?"

"Yes," she breathes.

Fuck it.

I'm driving to her house. We'll complete the mission

over the phone, and then maybe I can give her a kiss good-night. I would love nothing more than to kiss her tonight.

"What do you like about it?"

"The firefighter."

"What about him?"

"How he's annoyingly perfect."

I toggle to the app, approaching her place and turn on a different pulse setting. "What else do you like about him?"

"How he puts up with my shit."

I shake my head, considering everything and refocus on the mission at hand. "What do you like about the picture?"

"This guy is pretty hot." She giggles. "Blond hair, blue eyes, so strong."

"What do you wish he was doing to you?"

"Kissing me. Telling me he's going to make me come."

My chest rumbles. "One of these days the mission will be eight, and you will have to give me eight."

"I'll do my best, but—"

"The next time I tell you eight. It's eight."

"I'll do what I'm told," she breathes, and I hear how close she is.

"Good ... will you do what you're told right now?"

"Yes."

"You need to come outside and give me a kiss goodnight."

"What?"

Smirking, I hang up. *Let's see if she does this.*

Doubt creeps in as the seconds pass, but this was the right move. This is how we're going to get back on track. Her front light turns on, and I immediately step out of my truck.

"Claire," I exhale, seeing her in her doorway. She looks

as beautiful as ever with her messy bun, sweatpants and a T-shirt.

I pull her in by the back of her neck and kiss her deep. She wraps her arms around my neck, pressing her body into mine. I have missed every single thing about her. Running my hands down her back, I kiss her with more need. I squeeze her ass, lifting her for a moment, excited about what's next for us. Breaking our kiss, I hold her face in my hands. Staring at her, I take in everything, her blue eyes, freckles, red hair.

"I love you, Claire," I blurt out.

Her eyes widen.

"If this is all you're ready for, I will do this every fucking night with a smile on my face."

She starts to cry, and I probably shouldn't have said I loved her, but I couldn't hold it back any longer.

"Baby," I softly say, brushing the tears away. "I hate when you cry."

"Happy tears," she whispers, deeply inhaling.

I rest my hand on her heart, and she sets hers on mine. Without words, we begin breathing together. Inhaling and exhaling. Smiling and connecting.

After a few breaths, Claire says, "I'm ready to take you up on dinner and cookies."

"With Gabby?"

She nods.

I cup her face in my hands, kissing her deep. This is huge for us. She wants us. "Tell me when."

51

Claire

Wednesday, August 6th

"Where are your pink shoes?" I ask Gabby, not seeing them in our shoe organizer.

"Bear likes them," she calls from the living room, and I see the bear Jake got her is wearing the shoes.

"Tonight, when you meet the firefighter that got you this bear, tell him how much you like it and say thank you."

She nods.

So far, I've only said that we're having dinner with Jake, the guy daddy wasn't nice to, and the guy who bought the cookies. That I met him when there was a fire. That he's nice. But now ... I want to say this is mommy's boyfriend. But I should probably talk to Jake about that first. Right now, this is just dinner. I shake my head. He said he loves me, and I know it's the truth.

"Gabby, Jake is also mommy's boyfriend, so I'm excited for you to get to know him. We're going to be seeing more of him."

She nods, and it feels right. I want to be Jake Schmidt's girlfriend.

✩
✩
✩

Unbuckling Gabby from her booster seat, I hear Jake's voice. "Need any help?"

"All set."

Gabby and I walk hand in hand to his front door, where he stands in jeans and a T-shirt. *So casual,* I want to tease.

"Gabby, this is Jake."

"How many fires have you put out?" she asks.

He chuckles, shrugging. "Not that many. I spend more time helping people each day. Come in. I have surprises for both of you."

I tilt my head. He did not need to get us anything. We take our shoes off and follow him into the living room. I immediately spot a large, wicker basket filled with toys. That wasn't here the last time I was here.

"Here's where I keep my toys," he says, gesturing to the basket. "You can play with them whenever you're here." Then he hands Gabby a book. "Para ti." *For you.*

"¿Hablas Español?" Gabby asks, tilting her head.

"Si."

"¿Puedes leerme este libro en Español?" *Can you read the book in Spanish?* she skeptically asks. I internally laugh, seeing myself in her right now. Maybe my cynicism isn't the best trait for her to be picking up. But I am curious to know more about Jake's fluency.

"Puedo leer el libro en Español." *I can read the book in Spanish.*

202

"Leéme el libro en Español." *Read me the book in Spanish.*

I nudge her. "Por favor." *Please.*

"No question she's your daughter." Jake chuckles, taking a seat on the carpet. Gabby follows, taking a seat next to him and handing him the book. He easily reads the first couple of pages of the children's book, and I sit on the recliner watching them. *It's a story about bravery,* and I close my eyes, fighting back tears, happy ones.

He finishes the book and looks over at me. Now I'm crying. I wipe my face, and he steps toward me, pulling me in for a hug. "Jake," I breathe.

"Too much?"

"No." I take a deep breath, then playfully poke him. "How do you know Spanish?"

"The department paid for a year's worth of classes, and I kept taking them." Jake wraps his arm around my shoulder, squeezing me into him. I look over at Gabby, who has made herself at home, examining the toys Jake has.

Jake releases me, then steps toward the kitchen. After grabbing a few things from the fridge, he says, "Alright ladies, tonight we're having chicken tenders and steamed vegetables."

"What about the cookies?" Gabby asks as I make my way toward the kitchen, and I laugh softly to myself.

"Of course," Jake says, taking them out of a cabinet. "I couldn't forget about those."

"What can I help with?" I ask, now at his side.

"Nothing."

I raise my brow, and he steals a quick handful of my ass. "I want to take care of you two."

I know he's serious, more serious than anyone else will

ever be. I give in to the fact that he is never going to treat me like they did. He is not them. He is the one.

I grab for his hand, and he interlaces his fingers with mine, causing me to draw in a deep breath. "I'm ready to be your girlfriend if the offer is still on the table."

"It's on the table." He leans down, kissing me so sweetly. "I love you, girlfriend."

Staring into his eyes, I say what I'm thinking, "I love you, Jake."

52

Jake

One month later
Saturday, September 13th

"Thirty-five," Claire says, watching me as I drive us to dinner at my parents' house.

Squeezing Claire's thigh with a permanent smile on my face, I echo, "Thirty-five."

I always thought thirty-five would feel different. The version of my life I imagined at twenty-five involved a house, a wife, and a couple of kids by now.

One out of three. In baseball, that would still get me into the major leagues.

But this moment is better than I could have ever imagined. I didn't start this year thinking I'd find the one. I'd hoped for it, but I was beginning to lose hope. And there she was.

I used to want time to go by quicker, but now I want it to slow down.

Claire rests her hand over mine, her fingers tracing circles over my knuckles.

My girl.

It's too bad my other girl is with her dad this weekend. I look down at the bracelet she made me for my birthday. Tuesday night dinners with Claire and Gabby, and Wednesday date nights with Claire have been the best additions to my week. Every other weekend, Claire and I work on her stamina, and no matter what, I'm at her door each night once Gabby is down for a quick chat and a goodnight kiss.

I love my new schedule.

I love our life together.

I'm not rushing anything, but the thought of Claire as my wife and Gabby as my daughter already feels like a certainty. No matter the drama, no matter what comes our way, Claire isn't alone. She has me, and she has the best damn lawyer I've ever met.

When we get married, everything will shift. Our lives, our routines, our home—it won't just be mine anymore. It'll be ours. And I'm ready for that. Ready for the responsibility, the commitment, the permanence.

But tonight? Tonight isn't about what's coming. It's about this moment—introducing Claire to my parents for the first time.

"You ready?" I ask, squeezing her hand as I park in my parents' driveway.

"I've never been more ready."

Want to read more?

Hint: Claire getting to eight.
Scan the QR code or click here for bonus chapters.

https://dl.bookfunnel.com/1z482b3mkr

Want to read more?

Want to read more of Serena Pier's work?

High Five Novella Series
An interconnected, small town, holiday-themed novella
series with spice

Santa's Coming
Cupid's Shot
Shamrock Kisses
Run, Little Bunny
Falling for Red
Sharing Shadow Secrets (Releasing September 25, 2025th)

SAGA Series
A spicy coming of age series following the main character
through her twenties and endless personal and professional
ups and downs. Each book chronicles a different
relationship of hers until she gets her happily ever after in
The One.

The Townie – Prequel
The Renter – Book 1
The Client – Book 2
The Reporter – Book 3 (Releasing September 4th, 2025)
The One – Book 4 (Releasing in 2026)

Acknowledgments

A special thank you to my beta and sensitivity readers Aubrie, Britt, Clara, Denise, Hayley, Jayden, Jennie, Katherine, Kayla, KC, Kortni, Laura, Lauren, Marissa, Mary, Rachel, Steph, Steph M., & Terell!

Ella & Jenn, thank you for your help with the Spanish translations.

Thank you for the developmental editing support, Kayla W., Ashley O., and Emma! & Pauline for final proofing.

Shoutout to my TikTok Subscribers Alison, Cheyenne, Clara, Crystal, Danielle, Ella, Erin, Jayden, Jen, Jerrica, Joslyn, Jossimar, Kammie, Katie, Katherine, Katrina, Kayla, Kayla H., Kortni, Leanna, Mary, Michelle, Michelle S., Mikayla, Nayalee, Rhonda, Samantha, Shontain, Steph, and Sara.

About The Author

Serena Pier is a recovering girl boss, mom, and wife. After being called a brat for as long as she can remember, she decided to lean into it—writing sassy, strong, and complex female characters who fully embrace the sexy side of that word. Her books are influenced by her endless fascination with power dynamics and how they play out in relationships, workplaces, and everyday life. Most of her stories are set in and around Chicago, playing tribute to her Midwestern roots and love of all things dairy. When she isn't in front of a screen, Serena can be found pontooning with her family, enjoying a glass of wine with friends, and driving as fast as she can on the track.

Follow Serena Pier on TikTok & Instagram:
@SerenaPierWrites

To stay up to date with upcoming releases, join Serena Pier's newsletter:
https://serenapier.com/pages/newsletter

About The Author

Buy signed copies and Serena Pier merchandise here:
https://serenapier.com/

www.ingramcontent.com/pod-product-compliance
Ingram Content Group UK Ltd.
Pitfield, Milton Keynes, MK11 3LW, UK
UKHW021457040625

6237UKWH00035B/591